Damsel in Distress

Longarm stood there on the wharf, frozen by the threat to
Kate's life. There were three intruders, one with a hold of
Kate. Longarm breathed slowly and deeply. The glance over
his shoulder had told him that the two men on the boat had
guns drawn. He hoped the alcohol had taken its toll on them,
because a few yards away, Kate was struggling desperately
against the third attacker. She had managed to free her throat
from his grip, but he still held her with one hand, which Kate
clawed with both of hers.

Longarm surged to his feet and lunged toward the struggling
figures. He couldn't risk a shot, not with Kate pressed up so
tightly a

DON'T MISS THESE
ALL-ACTION WESTERN SERIES
FROM THE BERKLEY PUBLISHING GROUP

THE GUNSMITH *by J. R. Roberts*
Clint Adams was a legend among lawmen, outlaws, and ladies. They called him . . . the Gunsmith.

LONGARM *by Tabor Evans*
The popular long-running series about Deputy U.S. Marshal Long—his life, his loves, his fight for justice.

SLOCUM *by Jake Logan*
Today's longest-running action Western. John Slocum rides a deadly trail of hot blood and cold steel.

BUSHWHACKERS *by B. J. Lanagan*
An action-packed series by the creators of Longarm! The rousing adventures of the most brutal gang of cutthroats ever assembled—Quantrill's Raiders.

DIAMONDBACK *by Guy Brewer*
Dex Yancey is Diamondback, a Southern gentleman turned con man when his brother cheats him out of the family fortune. Ladies love him. Gamblers hate him. But nobody pulls one over on Dex . . .

WILDGUN *by Jack Hanson*
Will Barlow's continuing search for his daughter, kidnapped by the Blackfeet Indians who slaughtered the rest of his family.

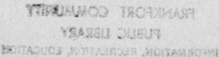

TABOR EVANS

LONGARM

AND THE YUKON QUEEN

JOVE BOOKS, NEW YORK

W
Pb
EVA

This is a work of fiction. Names, characters, places and incidents either
are the product of the author's imagination or are used fictitiously, and
any resemblance to actual persons, living or dead, business
establishments, events, or locales is entirely coincidental.

LONGARM AND THE YUKON QUEEN

A Jove Book / published by arrangement with
the author

PRINTING HISTORY
Jove edition / December 2001

All rights reserved.
Copyright © 2001 by Penguin Putnam Inc.
This book, or parts thereof, may not be reproduced in any form
without permission.
For information address: The Berkley Publishing Group,
a division of Penguin Putnam Inc.,
375 Hudson Street, New York, New York 10014.

Visit our website at
www.penguinputnam.com

ISBN: 0-515-13206-3

A JOVE BOOK®
Jove Books are published by The Berkley Publishing Group,
a division of Penguin Putnam Inc.,
375 Hudson Street, New York, New York 10014.
JOVE and the "J" design
are trademarks belonging to Penguin Putnam Inc.

PRINTED IN THE UNITED STATES OF AMERICA

10 9 8 7 6 5 4 3 2 1

Chapter 1

The girl's name was Glory. That was appropriate, thought Longarm as she stood nude before him, because she sure as hell was glorious.

She was young, no more than nineteen or twenty, and thick, straight blond hair hung around her deceptively innocent face and down her back. A little below medium height, she was solidly built, not fat but not slender either. Her full breasts rode high on her chest, round and firm and crowned with large brown nipples. Below her breasts, her belly was just slightly rounded and flowed smoothly into luxuriant hips. The thicket of fine-spun hair at the juncture of her thighs was a shade darker than that on her head. Her calves were muscular, and as she turned to let Longarm inspect her, he saw that her creamy rear end was perfectly rounded.

He was sprawled on his back on a San Francisco hotel room bed, not the fanciest place in the world, but a far cry from the worst. Glory had already undressed him, and the show she had put on for him while taking off her own clothes had stiffened his manhood until it jutted up from his groin, a long, thick pole of male flesh. Glory looked at it, licked her lips in a combination of anticipation and apprehension, and said, "You must think I'm pretty."

"Darlin'," Longarm said, "you look good enough to eat."

Glory clapped her hands together in delight. "Oh, good! I like that."

She ran over to the bed, threw herself down beside Longarm, and spread her thighs. He sat up and moved between her legs. She reached down and used her fingertips to peel back the rosy lips of her femininity. As Longarm leaned closer, he caught a whiff of clean, fresh woman scent, confirming what she'd told him earlier, that she'd had a bath before starting her evening's work in the Barbary Coast saloon where he'd met her.

"You don't mind licking it for a while before you stick that big ol' thing in me?" she asked.

"Nope." He bent over and replaced her fingers with his own, holding her open as his tongue reached out to slide along her slit and then circle the little bud of flesh at the top.

She put both hands on his head and pressed him even closer to her. Her hips began moving, and she panted out her passion as he probed and swooped and penetrated her core with his tongue. She was already wet and got even wetter as he worked her over with his mouth.

"You can . . . put a finger . . . in my ass . . . if you want," she said.

Longarm didn't mind. He reached under her with his right hand and found the puckered brown opening with the tip of his middle finger. Enough of her juices had already dribbled down there so that it was easy for him to slide his finger into the tight channel. He felt her muscles clamp down on it.

"Oh, my!" Glory said. "Oh, Custis!"

Back in the saloon, he had told her his name, Custis Long, but not his occupation, which happened to be Deputy United States Marshal. He had also bought her a drink or two and then suggested that they go upstairs. Glory had explained that the girls didn't have rooms upstairs, but had an arrangement whereby they could take gentlemen friends to the hotel next door. Longarm had told her that he always strove to be a gentleman and that he certainly hoped he could be her friend.

So they had wound up here in this room with the lamp

2

turned low, both of them stark naked and enjoying the hell out of each other.

It was almost a crime, Longarm reflected, that he got paid for this.

Glory's hips bucked up off the bed and her thighs clamped around Longarm's head, mashing his ears a little. She let out a yelp and then laughed as she thrust her femaleness against his face. After a minute she sagged back onto the mattress and opened her legs again, letting him breathe. He lifted his head and asked, "What was . . . so funny?"

"That mustache of yours . . . it tickles."

Longarm grinned. He was proud of the sweeping longhorn mustache, and sometimes it had added benefits besides being stylish.

"I've always figured that foolin' around ought to be fun. I like hearing a gal laugh."

She put a hand on his chest. "Lay down. It's your turn now. I won't be able to laugh much, though. My mouth's going to be full."

Longarm's shaft gave a little jump at the promising sound of that comment. He stretched out onto his back and Glory had him spread his legs so that she could sit between them. She took his heavy balls in one hand, cupping them and rolling them back and forth as she wrapped the fingers of her other hand around his pole as far as they would go. She began stroking it up and down as she fondled his sac.

"This is just about the prettiest talleywhacker I ever did see," she said as she stared at his organ. She milked a drop of fluid from the opening at the tip and used her thumb to spread it around over the head. When she had done that to her satisfaction, she leaned over and ran her tongue around the head.

Longarm's shaft throbbed. That was the sort of exquisite torment he couldn't endure for very long. Glory wrapped her lips around the thick pole and took as much of it as she could into her mouth. Her long blond hair fell around her face and spread like a blanket over Longarm's groin.

He withstood the sweet tenderness of her mouth as long

as he could, then urged her up over him. His shaft was drenched, and she was still very wet from what he had done to her earlier. So as she lowered her hips over his, he slipped into her with great ease. She slid down the pole until it was fully sheathed and hitting bottom. Then she began to ride hard, her hips pumping in a steady rhythm.

Longarm filled his hands with her firm breasts and strummed the erect nipples with his thumbs. Glory closed her eyes and caught her bottom lip between her teeth as she rode him at a passionate gallop. Both of them were more than ready when Longarm arched his hips up off the bed and began to spasm. His climax boiled up from his balls and exploded from his shaft, filling her with his seed. Glory cried out in fulfillment as shudders rolled through and shook her.

Finally, with one last thrust, Longarm expended the rest of what he had to give her. She fell forward, resting on his broad, hairy chest as his arms went around her. Her mouth was close to his ear, so that he felt the heat of her rapid breath as she tried to recover. Her breasts were flattened against his chest, and he could feel the thudding of her heart as well as his own.

"I . . . I never had it so good before, Custis," she said. "And that's not just whore talk. It's the truth."

"I'm glad you enjoyed yourself," he told her, "because I surely did." He ran his right hand down the smoothness of her back, then up the curve of her rump so that he could cup her left cheek and squeeze it. "I'm sure glad my pard told me to come see you."

She lifted her head a little. "Somebody recommended me? Who?"

There was the rub, as Shakespeare had said. Longarm wasn't sure what name the man he was looking for was using. He gambled and said, "Harrison."

Glory frowned down at him. "Who?"

Longarm put another name with the one he had given her. "Harrison Dodge." That was his quarry's real name. If Dodge was using some other moniker, Longarm might be out of luck. But he still had Dodge's description in reserve.

"Oh, you must mean Harry." Glory pushed herself into a sitting position again, still straddling Longarm's hips. "Little fella, kind of skinny, not much hair?"

Longarm smiled. "That's him."

And it was. The man Glory had just described fit Harrison Dodge's description right down to the ground.

"Well, I'll sure have to thank him when I see him again. For sending you to see me, I mean."

"Reckon I owe that old son some thanks, too," Longarm said. "You're a mighty fine gal, Glory. When do you think ol' Harrison'll be around again?"

"I don't know. It's been a couple of days. I thought I'd see him before now, since he came to the saloon three nights in a row." Glory smiled shyly. "He said he was coming back because of me."

Longarm didn't doubt that for a second. Harrison Dodge was right fond of short, blond, soiled doves. That was one thing Longarm knew for sure about him.

The other was that Dodge was part of one of the crookedest schemes to ever come down the pike.

"I didn't know his last name was Dodge, though," Glory went on with a slight frown. "He said his last name was Emerson."

"That's his middle name," Longarm said without hesitation. "Harrison Emerson Dodge is the full handle, but sometimes he whittles that down on account of it's such a mouthful."

Glory wiggled her hips, causing his still-embedded shaft to swell a little. "So are you."

Under other circumstances, Longarm wouldn't have minded a return engagement. Glory was damned good at what she did. But now he had work to do. He'd been in San Francisco for three days, searching through the saloons, bordellos, and gambling dens of the Barbary Coast for Harrison Dodge, and now that he was on the fugitive's trail at last, he figured he'd better move fast.

"You know, I ran into Harry in a restaurant, and he didn't

5

say where he was staying. He didn't happen to mention that to you, did he?"

"Sure, he's at the Cleveland House. I told him I'd come to see him there if he wanted, but he didn't think that was a good idea." Glory sighed. "I guess I ought to be used to it, being a soiled dove and all, but sometimes it still hurts when men don't want to be seen with me."

Longarm couldn't think of anything to tell her other than the hackneyed advice to marry one of her customers and give up whoring, and he didn't figure that would do any good. He said instead, "I'll go see him and have a talk with him."

Glory put a hand to her mouth. "Oh, don't get angry with him, Custis! I don't really blame him. And he's such a nice man."

"Well, I'll tell him to be extra nice to you next time he sees you." Which would be never if he had anything to say about it, Longarm thought. As soon as he got his hands on Harrison Dodge, Dodge was going on a train to Denver and ultimately back to Washington, D.C.

"That'll be fine, then." Glory wiggled her hips again. "Want to go one more time? It won't cost you any extra."

Longarm thought about it, then thought about his boss back in Denver, Chief Marshal Billy Vail. Vail wouldn't look kindly on it if he knew one of his deputies was playing slap-and-tickle with a whore instead of tending to business.

On the other hand, Longarm reflected as Glory leaned forward and kissed him, thrusting her tongue deep into his mouth, what Billy Vail didn't know wouldn't hurt him. . . .

"Damned old bones are killing me," Billy Vail had said a week earlier as he lowered himself into his chair in his office in Denver's federal building. "Sciatica's acting up something fierce." The balding, pink-faced lawman sighed. "Reckon I fell off too many horses, back in the days when I was riding with the Rangers."

Sitting in the red leather chair in front of the desk, Longarm nodded in sympathy as he puffed on a cheroot. He wasn't nearly as old as Vail, but he wasn't a spring chicken

anymore, either. Aches and pains took longer to go away these days. Of course, everything was relative. Compared to a lot of gents, he was in pretty good shape. His rangy, powerful frame was lean and hard, his wind was good despite all the cheroots he smoked, his eyesight was clear, and his hearing was as keen as ever. Nor had he had any complaints from his lady friends about any of his other abilities deteriorating. All in all, Longarm reflected, he was pretty well satisfied with life.

"I'm sending you after a federal fugitive," Vail said.

Longarm took the cheroot out of his mouth and blew a smoke ring, aiming it at the banjo clock on the wall of the office. He should have known his good mood wasn't going to last. Self-satisfaction was usually the first sign that things were about to go to hell in a hay wagon.

"What sort of fugitive, Billy?" Longarm asked.

"His name is Harrison Dodge." Vail took a sheet of paper from the pile that littered his desk and held it out toward Longarm. "There's his description."

Longarm took the paper and scanned the words on it. Harrison Dodge was thirty-five years old, five-feet-six-inches tall, and weighed 140 pounds. His hair, what was left of it, was dark brown and his eyes were brown, too. According to the document, until recently he had been employed as a clerk in the General Land Office of the Department of the Interior under Secretary Carl Schurz.

Longarm glanced up at Vail and said, "He don't sound like much of a desperado."

"Dodge is nothing by himself," Vail said. "He's just important because of what he knows."

"Which is what?"

"The identities of the higher-ups in one of the biggest swindles involving federal land that we've ever had to deal with."

Longarm sat up a little straighter. "The Interior Department's got rats nibbling around the edges, does it?"

Vail harrumphed. "Taking big bites is more like it," he said. "Dodge and other clerks in the General Land Office

7

have been altering documents so that federal land can be sold illegally. Not only that, but the same land is being sold more than once, and the suckers who buy it can't do anything about it because they know the whole deal is shady and they don't want to get in trouble with the government."

"No clerk came up with a scheme like that."

Vail shook his head. "No, it was somebody else's idea. Secretary Schurz has been trying to find out who came up with it, but he hasn't had any luck so far other than turning up Dodge. Senator Culp is putting a lot of pressure on Schurz to clean up this mess."

Longarm knew Senator Tobias Culp by reputation, but that was all. Culp, the senior senator from Pennsylvania, wielded a lot of power in the Senate, where he chaired the committee that oversaw the activities of the Interior Department. Longarm didn't find many things in the world more boring or depressing than politics, but he had to keep up with what was going on in Washington. Not to the extent that Vail did, of course, since Vail's job as chief marshal for the Western District was inherently more political.

Longarm tossed the description of Harrison Dodge back onto Vail's desk and said, "If they've got the goods on this fella, seems like they could get him to tell who else is mixed up in it in exchange for a lighter sentence."

"That's what Schurz figured on doing, until Harrison figured out somehow that his boss was onto him. Then he took off for the tall and uncut."

Longarm grunted. "So now it's our job to find him and bring him back."

"Secretary Schurz has requested the help of the Justice Department, that's right. He knows that Dodge left Washington on a westbound train."

"The West is a hell of a big place, Billy," Longarm pointed out.

Vail glared at him. "I've ridden as much of it as you have, so I reckon I know that. But we got lucky. Dodge left Washington with a ticket for Chicago, and in Chicago he bought another ticket, this one for San Francisco. He passed through

8

Denver two days ago—before we knew we were going to be looking for him."

Longarm winced. "That doesn't sound so lucky to me."

"At least we know where he's going. We know something else about him, too, something that Secretary Schurz was able to tell me."

"What's that?"

"He likes whores."

Longarm's eyebrows drew down in a frown. "What?"

"You heard me. Dodge can't seem to stay away from whores, especially a certain type. He likes them short and a mite on the chunky side, with blond hair."

That sounded all right to Longarm, but then, he liked just about all women, women of every shape and size and hair color, as long as they liked him.

"That's how whoever recruited him into the land fraud scheme got him to cooperate," Vail went on. "They had a prostitute in Washington working for them, and she had Dodge wrapped around her little finger."

"Then she'd know who was running things, too," Longarm said.

Vail shrugged. "She probably did, but she's dead. Another of her customers got too rough with her and busted her head. It was right after that that Dodge realized he was in trouble and ran. Bad luck all around. A day earlier and the authorities would've had both of them in custody and this mess might be cleared up now."

Longarm leaned forward to butt out his cheroot in a tin ashtray on Vail's desk, then settled back in the red leather chair. "So we know that Dodge was headed for San Francisco and that he likes short, blond soiled doves. That ain't a hell of a lot to go on, Billy."

"No, it's not," Vail agreed. "But it's what we've got, and we have to work with it. You find Dodge and bring him back here, Custis. If you do, I might let you take him all the way to Washington."

Longarm's eyes narrowed. He had been to Washington before and had no desire to go back. It was hot and sticky

9

and full of pompous windbags who usually had their hands out under the table. Washington was famous for its mosquitoes and other bloodsuckers.

"Do you want me to find this sumbitch or not, Billy?"

Vail frowned at him in confusion. "Of course I do."

Longarm took out another cheroot and bit off the end of it. "Then quit makin' threats."

He had gotten his travel vouchers from Henry, Billy Vail's pasty-faced clerk, and hoorawed him a little about how he was being sent to San Francisco to look for whores. Henry was the moralistic sort. He'd sniffed and said, "I shouldn't think that we'd have to pay you to do that. I can understand why Marshal Vail picked you for this assignment, however."

"Why's that?" Longarm had asked.

Henry sniffed again. "Send a degenerate to catch a degenerate."

Longarm had just grinned and strolled out of the office. He had a train to catch.

That train had taken him across the Rockies and the Sierra Nevadas to San Francisco, and several days of searching had finally led him to the blond prostitute called Glory. Glory, in turn, had told him where Harrison Dodge was staying.

So that was how Longarm came to find himself standing in front of the Cleveland House, an inexpensive hotel on the edge of the Barbary Coast. It was three stories tall and made of red brick, which meant it had probably been constructed after one of the great fires that had swept through this city by the bay, almost wiping it out. For a while after each of the conflagrations, most of the new buildings had been either brick or stone.

Longarm dropped the cheroot he was smoking and ground out the butt under the heel of his boot. He pulled down his vest and started across the street toward the front door of the hotel. In his brown tweed suit, sober vest, white shirt, string tie, and flat-crowned, snuff-brown Stetson, he knew he looked something like a businessman. The suit coat was cut so that it covered most of the Colt .45 Longarm carried in a

cross-draw rig on his left hip. A gold chain looped across his chest from one vest pocket to the other. At one end of the chain was a sizable pocket watch of the sort known as a turnip. A Colt .41 derringer was welded to the other end of the chain.

He opened the door and went into the lobby, which was mostly deserted at this time of the evening. A man in a derby hat sat in a chair next to a potted plant and flipped through the pages of a newspaper, obviously bored. Another man stood in front of the desk, talking to the clerk. As Longarm approached, he heard the clerk say, "Mr. Emerson is in Room 27."

"Thanks," said the man the clerk was talking to. He turned away from the desk and headed for the stairs.

Longarm never broke stride and never changed expression, though it required an effort not to do so. Emerson was the name Harrison Dodge had given Glory, and Longarm couldn't think of any other reason somebody would be looking for the fugitive clerk. All the instincts he had developed in his years as a lawman told him that something was wrong.

Longarm stepped up and rested his palms on the counter as the other man started up the stairs. "Can you tell me how to find Harley's Ballroom?" he asked the clerk, speaking loudly enough so that the man going up the stairs could hear him, too. Longarm knew that was the name of a dance hall down the street.

"Of course, sir," the clerk said. "Go back out through the front door, turn left, and continue along the street for three blocks. The establishment you're seeking will be on the right-hand side of the street."

Longarm nodded. "Much obliged." He turned and walked out of the lobby, not hurrying but not wasting any time, either. He turned left along the sidewalk just as the clerk had said.

As soon as he was past the lobby window, he broke into a run.

The mouth of an alley loomed on his left. He ducked into it, drawing his gun as he did so. Longarm moved quickly

11

along the alley, looking for a side entrance to the hotel. There wasn't one. There had to be some rear stairs, though, and as Longarm turned the corner of the building, he spotted them in the dimness of the lane that ran behind the hotel. When he reached them, he started up, moving with a speed and stealth that were unusual in such a big man.

Room 27 would be on the third floor if the Cleveland House numbered its rooms like most hotels. When Longarm reached the door at the top of the outside stairs, he tested the knob with his left hand. It turned. He thrust the door open.

Unfortunately, the hinges on the door hadn't been oiled in a long time, and they squealed like banshees in Hell. That drew the attention of the man standing in front of one of the rooms, gun drawn and foot upraised, ready to smash the heel of his boot into the lock. As the man's head snapped around toward Longarm, the big lawman recognized him as the one who had been asking downstairs about Emerson.

"Hold it!" Longarm snapped as he leveled his gun.

The man ignored the warning. He pivoted toward Longarm and jerked up his gun. Flame geysered from the muzzle as he triggered a shot. But the man's awkward position with his foot lifted threw him off balance, and he staggered slightly as he fired. The bullet whipped past Longarm's head.

Longarm didn't want to kill this man. He had too many questions that needed answers. He was about to try to drill the son of a bitch through the shoulder—

When something hit him hard from behind and knocked him sprawling forward.

Chapter 2

The gun in Longarm's hand bucked against his palm as he fell. In the close confines of the hotel corridor, the sound of the shot was deafening, as the report of the other man's gun had been. Longarm landed hard on the threadbare carpet runner, knocking the breath out of his lungs.

As he gasped for air, he rolled over. A gun blasted, sending a bullet into the floorboards where Longarm had been a second earlier. He saw a figure looming over him and kicked out at it. His heel landed solidly against the knee of the man who had knocked him down. The man howled in pain and staggered against the wall, slapping his free hand against it for support. The momentary respite gave Longarm the chance to recognize him as the man who had been leafing through the newspaper downstairs in the lobby.

Longarm hadn't forgotten the man who had been about to kick down the door of Dodge's room, but there was no time to deal with him now. Lying propped up on his left elbow, Longarm tipped up the barrel of his Colt and fired again, just as the man who had hit him from behind recovered his balance and triggered another shot. The slug from Longarm's gun ripped into the man's lower belly, traveling upward at a sharp angle since Longarm was lying on the floor. The would-be killer's bullet tore another hole in the carpet runner six inches from Longarm's side.

13

The gunman doubled over, firing a third and final shot, but this one went into the floor at his feet. His finger had clenched on the trigger of the revolver as Longarm's bullet bored through his guts. He toppled over, blood welling from the wound.

Longarm twisted around and came up on one knee as he turned toward Dodge's room. He saw to his surprise that the other gunman was lying in front of the door in a pool of blood. Longarm's aim had been thrown off when he was hit from behind, and the bullet intended for the man's shoulder had smashed into his throat instead.

Longarm surged to his feet. His face was grim. The air in the corridor reeked of burned gunpowder and the coppery smell of fresh blood. All the doors along the hallway were closed. The hotel's guests were probably hiding under their beds after what must have sounded to them like a small war had broken out in the corridor.

The door of Room 27 was closed, too. A couple of long strides brought Longarm to it. He kicked it open, the blow from his powerful leg slamming the door back against the wall of the room, and stepped fast to the side in case anyone inside the room tried to ventilate him. "Dodge!" Longarm shouted. "I'm a federal lawman! Come out with your hands up!"

A quavery, terrified voice came from inside the room. "Don't shoot! For God's sake, don't shoot!"

Longarm backed away from the door, his gun leveled. Even if Dodge wasn't the same sort as the gunslinging outlaws Longarm usually went after, he was still a fugitive and not to be trusted. "Come out where I can see you, and your hands better be empty, old son."

A moment later a short, slender figure appeared in the doorway. Harrison Dodge looked just like his description, except that at the moment he was extremely pale and his eyes were wide with fright. He had both hands raised to shoulder level.

"Don't shoot!" he said again as he emerged from the hotel room. "Please, I . . . I don't want any trouble." He glanced

down at the body lying at his feet and realized that the pool of blood from the man's ruined throat had almost reached his boots. Dodge moved skittishly away from the crimson puddle.

It was only a matter of time until the San Francisco law showed up in response to reports of what sounded like a massacre on the third floor of the Cleveland House. Longarm wasn't worried about dealing with the local badges. He had a badge of his own, along with his other bona fides in a leather folder inside his coat, and he had worked in San Francisco before and had friends on the police force.

But it was bound to get a mite confusing straightening out all this carnage, so before the coppers arrived Longarm wanted to get Harrison Dodge squared away. With his free hand he reached inside his coat for the pair of handcuffs he carried there. Once he had the cuffs on Dodge he could holster his gun.

"Come on over here, Dodge," he said. "You're under arrest."

"But . . . but I didn't do anything!"

"That'll be for somebody else to sort out, not me." Longarm motioned with the barrel of the Colt. "Come on. You look like the peaceable sort, so let's keep it that way."

"Y-yes, sir." With his hands still up, Dodge edged along the hallway toward Longarm. "Just don't h-hurt me."

Longarm didn't plan on hurting the mousy little fella, but he didn't say that. He just held the revolver and the handcuffs and waited.

Suddenly, Dodge's eyes got even wider as he looked past Longarm, and he yelped, "Look out!"

Longarm wasn't going to fall for that old trick. But then he heard the unmistakable metallic ratcheting of a gun being cocked.

He spun around and saw that the man he'd shot in the belly wasn't dead after all. In fact, the son of a bitch had managed to get hold of the gun he'd dropped and push himself up on one hand so that he could point the revolver shakily at Longarm. Longarm fired before the wounded gunman

15

could pull the trigger. The man's head jerked back as a black hole appeared in the center of his forehead. He slumped down on his face, dead beyond a shadow of a doubt this time because Longarm's bullet had taken off the back half of his head as it exploded out of his skull.

Longarm lowered the Colt and was about to swing around toward Dodge when something crashed heavily into the back of his head. The blow was brutal and unexpected, and it dropped Longarm to his knees. Darkness closed in around him as he felt himself falling forward.

Valiantly, he fought off unconsciousness as it tried to claim him. He was aware that he had dropped his gun. He felt around but couldn't find it. Gun or no gun, he figured he'd better get back to his feet. He pushed himself to his hands and knees and then came upright. He was dizzy. The corridor seemed to be spinning and looping in all sorts of crazy, impossible ways. Placing a hand against the wall to steady himself, he gave a little shake of his head, but instead of clearing away the cobwebs that just made things worse. So did closing his eyes.

So he opened them and looked around. For a second, his stunned brain wasn't sure who or what he was looking for, but then he remembered Harrison Dodge. Hard as it was to believe, it must have been Dodge who'd hit him. No one else had been in the corridor.

For a little fella, Dodge packed a wallop. Longarm wondered what Dodge had used to clout him.

Longarm's blurry eyes found his gun lying on the carpet runner. He bent to pick it up, almost fell again, then straightened slowly. He took a deep breath and swallowed the sick feeling in his throat. The door of Room 27 was still open. He stepped over to it, sweeping the Colt from side to side to cover anybody who might be inside.

But the room was empty. Dodge was gone.

Longarm looked down at the floor and saw that someone had run through the pool of blood. Gory footprints led down the hall toward the rear stairs. Dodge hadn't been so squeamish about stepping in the blood while he was making his

16

getaway. Longarm started after him, figuring that Dodge couldn't be more than a couple of minutes ahead of him.

"Hold it! Drop that gun, mister! *Now!*"

Longarm looked over his shoulder and saw a couple of blue-uniformed San Francisco coppers at the head of the main staircase. Both of them had their guns drawn, and they were young and probably inexperienced. That was a damned deadly combination, Longarm knew.

"Take it easy, gents," he said. He lifted his hands, still holding the Colt in the right one, and turned slowly toward the policemen. "We're on the same side. I'm a lawman, too."

"Drop the gun!" one of the coppers yelled.

Frustration and impatience gnawed at Longarm. The longer he had to mess with these babes in the woods, the more chance Harrison Dodge would have to get away from him. But if he didn't cooperate, the young officers might start blazing away at him. If he was dead, he sure couldn't catch Dodge, and anyway, how would it look if he let himself get gunned down by a pair like these two?

Carefully, he bent over and placed the Colt on the floor, then stood up again to back away from it. "Name's Custis Long," he told the two policemen as they advanced warily toward him. "I'm a deputy U.S. marshal. If you'll just let me reach inside my coat, I'll show you my bona fides."

"Do it slow," one of the coppers warned him. "If you try anything funny, we'll shoot."

Longarm didn't see anything funny about this situation. Harrison Dodge was putting distance between himself and Longarm with each passing second. Longarm took out the leather folder and opened it to reveal his badge and identification papers.

"One of your detectives will vouch for me, a fella named Ryan. And a couple of U.S. Treasury agents who work out of the San Francisco office know me, too. Their names are O'Hanlon and Coletti."

"That looks like a real marshal's badge," one of the coppers said dubiously.

"I think he must be telling the truth," the other one said.

Longarm suppressed the urge to let out a sulfurous curse. He put the folder away and said, "All right if I pick up my gun?"

One of the officers shrugged. "Yeah, go ahead." He looked around at the two sprawled, bloody corpses. "What the hell happened here?"

Longarm picked up his gun and his hat, which had fallen off during the fracas. "I was in pursuit of a federal fugitive. So were these two."

"Are they marshals, too?"

Longarm shook his head. "From the looks of it, they wanted the fella dead, while I just wanted to arrest him. That one there had his gun out and was about to kick down the door of that room. I got the drop on him, but then the other one hit me from behind. Things got a mite hectic after that."

"I'd say so. What about the fugitive?"

"Got away. I was about to slap the cuffs on him when one of these fellas turned out not to be quite so dead after all. While I was dealing with him, the one I'm after fetched me a knock on the head and lit a shuck."

"You don't talk like any federal lawman I ever saw," said the other copper. "You sound more like a cowboy."

Longarm's jaw clenched. He wasn't just about to waste time explaining to these wet-behind-the-ears officers that he had done a considerable amount of cowboying when he had first come to the frontier from West-by-God Virginia after the Late Unpleasantness. Instead he holstered his Colt and said, "I got to find that fella I'm after."

Before the coppers could argue with Longarm, the desk clerk from downstairs appeared at the landing and asked nervously, "Is . . . is everything all right up—Oh, my God!" The clerk had caught sight of the bodies.

Longarm strode past the officers toward the clerk. "The gent in Room 27, Emerson, did he have any bags?"

"Just . . . just one valise, if I remember correctly," the clerk replied. He was still staring past Longarm at the corpses. If he recognized Longarm from their brief encounter downstairs earlier, he gave no sign of it.

18

So Dodge was traveling light, Longarm thought. That was to be expected. But where would he go? Dodge had to feel that San Francisco was no longer safe for him, so he would try to get out of town as quickly as possible.

"Is there a train leaving tonight?"

Longarm had to ask the question again before the stunned clerk would answer it. "No, I don't think so. The next train doesn't leave until in the morning."

Longarm felt a little relief. That might give him a chance to locate Dodge.

"But there's a ship sailing tonight," the clerk added.

Longarm stiffened. "A ship?"

"That's right. I believe it's due to sail at eleven o'clock."

Longarm didn't ask where the ship was bound. Any destination would probably look pretty appealing to Harrison Dodge right about now.

He pushed past the clerk and started downstairs. One of the coppers called, "Hey! Come back here!" but Longarm ignored him. He didn't think the two youngsters would shoot him in the back, and he didn't have any more time to squander here.

His brain was working furiously as he went through the lobby and out of the hotel. The man who had been pretending to read the paper in the lobby had served as lookout for the one who'd been about to break into Dodge's room. The fella must have been just suspicious enough to follow Longarm out of the hotel and had seen him enter the alley. From there he had followed Longarm up to the third floor of the hotel and jumped him.

The lookout would have gone into the hotel first and pretended not to know the second man when he showed up. They had been professionals, Longarm realized, hired killers who had worked together before.

There was only one conclusion to draw from that.

For the moment, Longarm left it at that. He was heading for the docks along San Francisco Bay as fast as his long legs would take him. It had taken him a good ten minutes to get away from the coppers and the desk clerk, which meant

that Dodge had approximately a quarter-hour lead. Still, Longarm had a chance to get to the docks before the ship sailed. He could still stop Dodge—assuming, of course, that the fugitive was trying to leave San Francisco by boat, and that seemed to be his only option tonight, short of renting a horse and riding away. Dodge didn't seem to be the type to do that. He was a city boy.

As Longarm hurried down a steep hill toward the harbor, he took out his pocket watch and flipped it open, glancing at the face in the light from a saloon he passed. His mouth tightened grimly as he saw that it was exactly eleven o'clock already. He put the watch away and broke into a trot.

Ships didn't always depart right on schedule. This one might be a few minutes late weighing anchor. And a few minutes was all that Longarm needed.

He reached the street that ran along the waterfront and started running as he caught sight of sails in the harbor. He came up to an empty pier with a small shed at the foot of it. A lantern was burning in the shed.

Longarm stuck his head in and saw a man in uniform sitting at a tiny desk, writing something in a notebook. "That ship in the harbor," Longarm said, "did it just sail from here?"

The man looked up. The cap on his head had lettering on it that read H-M SHIPPING LINES. He said, "That's right. You're too late, mister. Did you have a ticket?"

Longarm shook his head.

"Then you wouldn't have been able to sail on her anyway. I just sold the last available space not five minutes before the ship weighed anchor."

Longarm held out a hand at shoulder height. "To a little fella about this tall, carrying a valise?"

"That's right. A friend of yours?"

"Not hardly," Longarm said. He stepped out of the shed and peered out over the harbor. In the moonlight, he could still see the sails of the vessel that had just left, carrying with it Harrison Dodge. The sails had caught the wind, and the

ship was heading for the Golden Gate and the open sea. There would be no catching it now.

Longarm looked back over his shoulder at the shipping line clerk. "Where's that boat bound?"

"You don't know?"

"Wouldn't be asking if I did," Longarm said.

"Sorry. But to answer your question, mister, that's the *Stansfield*, bound for the port of St. Michael."

"Where the hell's that?"

"Alaska Territory."

Longarm looked out in the harbor again. The sails had dwindled until they were out of sight.

Alaska. Seward's Folly. One of the biggest damned chunks of icy wilderness in the world.

Son of a bitch, thought Longarm.

San Francisco was a cosmopolitan city. The Western Union office stayed open twenty-four hours a day. Longarm sent a telegram to Billy Vail, then headed back to the hotel where he was staying. The place was similar to the Cleveland House in that it was inexpensive, but it was in a little better neighborhood.

Longarm made one more stop along the way. He went into a saloon and bought a bottle of Maryland rye. His head ached from being hit. When he got back to his hotel room, he took a couple of slugs of the whiskey, then undressed down to his long underwear, propped a chair under the door knob, and hung his gunbelt on the bedpost where the Colt would be handy. He crawled into bed and fell asleep within seconds after his head hit the pillow.

He woke early the next morning, shaved, dressed, and went downstairs to the hotel dining room for breakfast. The matronly waitress took his order and brought a pot of coffee and a cup and saucer to get him started. Longarm had finished one cup by the time the steak and eggs and flapjacks arrived. The food and coffee drove away the last vestiges of

21

the headache and he was pretty close to being himself again as he walked over to the telegraph office.

His wire to Vail had been simple on the surface of it: he had described his near miss at arresting Harrison Dodge and told how the two gunmen he'd been forced to kill were after Dodge. Longarm knew that Vail would understand what that meant. Dodge represented a great threat to whoever was behind the land-fraud scheme, and that mastermind must have sent the hired killers after him. Dodge was on the run not only from the law but also from his former employer.

Longarm had closed the message by saying that Dodge was now a passenger on the *Stansfield*, bound for St. Michael, Alaska Territory, and asked Vail for further orders. It was possible Vail had already replied, Longarm thought as he went into the Western Union office, since Denver was an hour ahead of San Francisco and Vail usually showed up quite early at the federal building, where the message from Longarm had been waiting.

A different clerk was on duty now. Longarm identified himself, and the man said, "Oh, yes, Marshal Long. I have a message for you. It's right here."

The clerk picked up a yellow telegraph flimsy and passed it through the window in the counter to Longarm. Vail's message was short and to the point.

> FOLLOW AND ARREST DODGE NO MATTER
> WHERE STOP ALL EXPENSES AUTHORIZED
> STOP VAIL CHIEF MARSHAL.

Well, that was that, Longarm thought as he tucked the message into his coat pocket. It looked like he was going to Alaska.

"Any reply, Marshal?" the clerk asked.

Longarm considered for a moment, then shook his head. "Nope." There was nothing else to say. He had thought about advising Vail to check into the death of that prostitute back in Washington, D.C., who had been involved with Dodge, but he knew Vail would do that on his own. Longarm sus-

pected the woman's death hadn't been just a case of a customer getting too rough, as Vail had said. More than likely the same man who wanted Dodge disposed of had ordered that the woman be killed, too. With the land-fraud scheme collapsing, the man behind it was trying to cover all his tracks.

Longarm left the telegraph office and walked toward the harbor. It was a typical San Francisco day, cloudy and cool even though it was summer. It would probably rain later, Longarm thought.

He went to the dock where the *Stansfield* had departed the night before. Just as in the telegraph office, a different man was on duty in the shed that housed the office of the H-M Shipping Lines. He asked Longarm, "What can I do for you, friend?"

"When's the next boat heading for Alaska?"

The man grinned. "Got the gold fever, do you?"

Longarm hesitated. He didn't know a whole hell of a lot about Alaska. The fur trapping was supposed to be pretty good up there, he'd heard. If people were going up there looking for gold, though, that might make a good cover story for him.

"That's right," he said. "I reckon I do."

"Well, I don't know if you'll find any or not, but I'll be glad to sell you a ticket. The *Bowman* sails next week."

Longarm swallowed a groan of disappointment. A week was a long time. If Dodge got to Alaska a whole week ahead of him, that would make it that much more difficult to find the fugitive. But there didn't seem to be a damned thing Longarm could do about it.

"Bound for what port?" he asked.

"St. Michael."

That clenched it. The next ship was going the same place Dodge had gone. Now Longarm didn't have any choice. "I'll take a ticket," he said, digging in his pocket for money.

The shipping clerk started writing out the ticket. "You have an outfit yet?" he asked. "If you do, you'll need cargo space. A mule, or anything like that?"

Longarm took a chance, basing his answer on what he knew of prospectors and prospecting in other parts of the country. "Nope. Figured to get outfitted once I got there."

"That's a wise move, friend. It'll save you some money on the voyage, and there are plenty of places in St. Michael that can take care of you. Gold hunting is going to be big business in Alaska one of these days. Mark my word on it."

Longarm didn't argue the point, figuring that he didn't know enough to do so. He took the ticket the clerk gave him and paid over the money for it, which seemed a mite exorbitant. But Billy Vail's telegram had been specific: *All expenses authorized.* Henry might quibble about it out of habit, but sooner or later the Justice Department would wind up paying for this ticket and anything else Longarm had to buy when he got to St. Michael.

He noted the day and time of departure written on the ticket, then nodded and said, "Much obliged."

"There's one thing I'd do before the ship sails, if I was you," the clerk said.

"What's that?"

"Buy some warmer clothes. Even the summers in Alaska Territory can be pretty cold, I hear."

Longarm said, "Thanks. I'll do that."

As he walked back to his hotel, he reflected that he would probably pick up a rifle and some more ammunition, too. He might not run into any more hired killers gunning for Harrison Dodge, but if he did, he wanted to be ready.

He walked into the hotel lobby, intending to get his key and go right up to his room, but two men stood up from the chairs where they had been sitting and moved to intercept him. Longarm tensed, then relaxed a little as he recognized one of the men, a tall, raw-boned, lantern-jawed gent with red hair. His name was Ryan.

The San Francisco Police Department had come to call.

Chapter 3

Ryan didn't smile at Longarm as he said, "Hello, Marshal."

"Ryan," Longarm said. He put out a hand. "Good to see you again."

The San Francisco detective shook his hand but still didn't smile. "But not so good that you came by the office to let me know that you were in town."

Longarm shrugged. "I'm here on federal business. Didn't see any need to bring you local fellas in on it."

"Even though we might have been able to help you?"

"I'm used to playing a lone hand," Longarm said.

The other man, chunky and red-faced, stepped forward, his chin thrust out belligerently. "Your 'lone hand' got two men killed mister. What do you have to say to that?"

Ryan lifted a hand to hold the other man back and said, "Take it easy, Walton. I've worked with Marshal Long before. You start pushing him and he'll just get his back up."

Longarm took out a cheroot and put it unlit in his mouth. "I didn't mean to step on anybody's toes," he said around the cigar. "And as for those two fellas I shot last night, they were doing their damnedest to kill me at the time." He inclined his head toward the stairs. "If we have to talk about this, the lobby ain't the best place. Come on up to my room."

Ryan hesitated, then nodded. "All right. Come on, Walton."

The other detective came along, but his expression made it clear he didn't care for the idea—or for Longarm. Once they reached Longarm's room, the big federal lawman picked up the bottle of Tom Moore from the top of the wardrobe and asked his two visitors if they'd like a drink.

"It's barely ten o'clock in the morning," Walton said, frowning at him in disgust.

"You know what the sailors say about the sun being over the yardarm somewhere in the world."

"Well, it isn't here," Walton snapped.

"Put the whiskey away, Long," Ryan said patiently. "Then tell us what brings you to our town and how come you're going around shooting some of our other visitors."

"Those two weren't from these parts?" Longarm asked.

Ryan shook his head. "No one could identify them. As far as we can tell, they're strangers to San Francisco."

"Doesn't surprise me," Longarm said. "Somebody hired them and sent 'em after the same man I'm looking for."

"And who might that be?"

Longarm considered the question, then said, "All I can tell you is that he's a federal fugitive." Billy Vail hadn't specifically ordered him to keep Dodge's identity a secret, but in light of the fact that the crime in which Dodge was involved might go all the way to the highest levels of power in Washington, it might be better to be discreet.

"That's not good enough," Walton said. "You'd better give us some details, Long, or by God, we'll lock you up so fast—"

Ryan turned on him and said, "Damn it, Walton, I told you to take it easy. I'm in charge of this investigation, not you."

Calmly, as the two policemen glared at each other, Longarm took out a lucifer, snapped it into life on an iron-hard thumbnail, and lit a cheroot. He puffed on it to get it going good, then inhaled deeply as he dropped the match into the bucket by the bed. Longarm blew a smoke ring and said, "If you want more details, I reckon you can wire my boss Billy Vail back in Denver. I've said about all I'm going to say."

"What about the two dead men?" Walton shot at him.

Longarm shrugged. "They were trying to kill the fella I'm after, like I said. One of them was about to bust down the gent's door when I got the drop on him. But then the other one jumped me from behind. Hell, if I'd had a chance, I would have taken one or both of them alive. I've got some questions myself I want answers to."

"All right," Ryan said. "There won't be any charges brought in those killings. Will you be here for the inquest?"

"If it's during the next week, I will be."

Walton said, "You're staying in San Francisco?"

"For a few days," Longarm replied. He drew on the cheroot again.

"This man you're looking for," Ryan said, "do you know what happened to him?"

Longarm hesitated again. He trusted Ryan, having worked with the man before, but Walton was an unknown quantity. It seemed highly unlikely that Walton could have any connection with Harrison Dodge or the killers who might still be after him, but Longarm wasn't prepared to take that chance.

"The little bastard got away," he said. "I don't know if I'll be able to find him again or not, but I have to try."

"You don't have any leads?" Ryan asked.

Longarm shook his head and lied. "Nope. But that don't mean I'll give up."

Ryan sighed. "All right, then. Since you won't be leaving this jurisdiction until after the inquest, I guess we're done with you. But I'm warning you, Long—I don't want the town filling up with corpses like it did the last time you came to San Francisco."

"I'll do my best to oblige."

"See that you do. Come on, Walton."

Walton followed Ryan out of the room, giving Longarm a narrow-eyed, unfriendly stare over his shoulder as he did so. Longarm closed the door, glad that he'd had to lie only a little to the police.

Unlike Ryan and Walton, he knew that there was no point

in searching for Harrison Dodge in San Francisco. Despite that, however, he was going to have to make a show of doing so for the next few days.

That was all right, he told himself. It would give him a chance to see Glory again. . . .

She was on all fours, her blond head resting on a pillow, her round, delectable rear end poked high in the air. "Do me this way, Custis," she said.

Longarm stood naked beside the bed and eyed approvingly the stance Glory had taken. He had a good view of the plump, pink lips of her femininity, topped by the tight opening between the widespread cheeks of her ass. He tickled that orifice with the tip of his finger, making her wiggle her hips. "Sure you don't want me to cornhole you?"

"Later," Glory gasped. "Right now just do it the usual way. And hurry!"

Longarm's massive shaft was fully erect, standing out in front of him like a battering ram. He moved closer and teasingly ran the tip of it up and down the folds of Glory's sex. She pushed her hips back at him, and he watched as the head of his organ slipped into her.

He put his hands on her hips to hold her in position and keep her from engulfing him all the way. He moved slightly, sliding another inch inside her.

"Oh, you're killing me, Custis!" Glory cried. "I want it all inside me!"

"We're gettin' there," he assured her. "I thought you gals liked to make it last as long as possible."

"Sometimes . . . that's right," she said. "But right now . . . I just want you . . . to do me!"

"Always try to oblige a lady." Longarm drove forward with his hips, burying the entire length of his throbbing shaft inside her velvety sheath.

Glory muffled a scream of pleasure by biting into the pillow under her head. Longarm tightened his grip on her hips and surged in and out of her. If he hadn't had hold of her, she would have been pushed halfway across the bed by the

emphatic strokes. He had to clench his jaw to keep from yelling out his own excitement.

With each forward thrust, he filled her, reaching as far into her as he could go. After several minutes that found them both breathless and covered with a fine sheen of sweat, they were ready to let their climaxes sweep over them. Glory panted, "Now, Custis, now!"

He pushed into her a final time and held himself steady, loving the soft pressure of her rump against his groin. A shudder of culmination went through him, and the thick, sticky seed began to burst from him and fill her wet, heated cavern. He was unable to hold back the low, hoarse cry that came from his throat.

When he was finished emptying himself into her, he let go of her hips and she slumped forward, his softening organ slipping wetly out of her. She breathed heavily as she sprawled facedown on the bed. Equally breathless, Longarm lay down beside her on his back.

"That was . . . even better than . . . the other time," Glory said, her voice muffled by the fact that she still had her face pressed into the pillow. "You're really . . . something, Custis."

"So are you," he told her. He reached over and moved one of the wings of blond hair out of the way so that he could see the side of her face. In profile like this, and in satisfied repose, her features looked very young. Longarm thought again that she ought to give up this profession and settle down, but it wasn't his place to be telling anybody what to do with her life.

She moved over on the bed so that she could press her hip to his. "I just wish Harry would come around again so I could show him how glad I am he told you about me. Have you seen him since you were here last time?"

Longarm had planned to bring up Harrison Dodge, but Glory had saved him the trouble. Grateful for that, he said, "Yeah, I saw him, but not for long. Hate to say it, Glory, but I reckon he's left town."

She lifted her head and her lips pursed in a pout. "Without saying good-bye to me?"

"He was in a mite of a hurry," Longarm said. "Some sort of business deal."

"Well, he'd better come see me the next time he's in San Francisco. You tell him that if you run into him, hear?"

"I sure will," Longarm promised. He paused for a moment, then asked, "Say, nobody else has been asking about old Harry, have they?"

"No, why would they? Does he have other friends here in town?"

Not friends, thought Longarm, but there might still be enemies out there searching for Harrison Dodge. Longarm had no way of knowing if the man behind the land-fraud scheme was aware yet that his first two emissaries had failed. The man might be waiting for the hired killers to report back to him that Dodge was dead. If that was the case, Longarm had something of a respite.

But it wouldn't last forever. Sooner or later, when the first two gunmen didn't come back, the man who had hired them would send out more killers. For all Longarm knew, that might have happened already. That was why he asked Glory if anyone else had contacted her looking for Harrison Dodge.

"Nope, not that I know of," he said in answer to her question. "But you never can tell when you'll run into somebody you know. Sometimes it seems like the bigger the country grows, the smaller it gets at the same time."

She sighed. "I know. Things sure aren't like they were when I was a kid."

Hearing a statement like that from someone so blatantly young made Longarm want to laugh, but he suppressed the impulse. Instead he said, "I'll still be in town a few more days myself. Mind if I come see you again?"

She rolled so that she was facing him and reached over to grasp his manhood. It began to harden again at the soft touch of her fingers. "You'd damned well better," Glory said as Longarm's shaft swelled to fill the palm of her hand.

*   *   *

As nice as romping with Glory was, Longarm had other things on his mind during his stay in San Francisco. There was the inquest into the deaths of the two men in the third-floor corridor of the Cleveland House, for one. It was a simple affair, attended only by the coroner, the coroner's jury, the hotel clerk, the two young police officers who had been the first badges to arrive after the shooting, Detectives Ryan and Walton, and Longarm. Longarm told his story without going into any details about the federal fugitive he was pursuing. He hoped that the coroner wouldn't ask any awkward questions. He could always refuse to answer them, but Billy Vail liked for his deputies to cooperate with the local authorities whenever possible.

Ryan must have had a talk with the coroner ahead of time, because the man asked only a few innocuous questions and then the jury brought in twin verdicts of justifiable homicide by a duly sworn officer of the law in performance of his duties. That closed the books on the deaths of the two men, neither of whom had ever been identified.

After the inquest, Ryan came up to Longarm in the lobby of the courthouse and said, "Well, that's it. You're free to go, Marshal."

Longarm nodded. "Don't worry. I'll be leaving town in a day or two."

"You haven't shot anybody since the last time I saw you?"

"Been as quiet and peaceful as a little church mouse," Longarm replied with a grin.

Ryan grunted. "That'll be the day, when Custis Long is quiet and peaceful." He jerked his head toward Walton, who was waiting on the other side of the lobby. "My partner over there would like nothing better than to arrest you and lose the key, so you'd best watch your step the rest of the time you're here."

"I intend to," Longarm said. "All I figure to do is a little shopping."

He attended to that later in the day, going into one of San Francisco's large emporiums to buy some denim trousers, a couple of flannel shirts, and a jacket lined with sheepskin.

He had all those items back in Denver, but they wouldn't do him a lick of good there. In addition to the clothes, he bought a Winchester rifle and several boxes of ammunition for it and his Colt. With that taken care of, he picked up some jerky and dried fruit, since he would be expected to provide much of his own food during the sea voyage to Alaska. The trip would take several weeks, since the ship would have to circle around the Aleutian Islands and approach the Alaskan coast from the southwest. However, St. Michael was located at the mouth of the Yukon River, which provided a quicker and easier route to the territory's interior, as opposed to the back-breaking, overland route from farther south. Anyway, that didn't really matter to him, Longarm reflected, since he wasn't really going to Alaska to look for gold. The only thing he was after was Harrison Dodge.

Glory pouted when he visited her on his last night in San Francisco. "I'm going to miss you so much, Custis," she said as they lay together after making love for the final time. "You'll come see me the next time you're in town, won't you?"

"You've got my word on that," he told her. His arm was around her shoulders. He tightened the embrace and kissed the top of her head as she rested it on his shoulder. He knew better than to get sentimental about a girl like Glory, who would probably be in bed with at least one other gent before the night was over, but he felt some real fondness for her anyway. Without her help, he might not have found Harrison Dodge, and it sure wasn't her fault that Dodge had gotten away from him.

Unlike the *Stansfield*, which had sailed at night, the *Bowman* weighed anchor and left the dock in the middle of the day. Longarm went aboard a half-hour before the ship departed. His eyes studied the people on the crowded docks. No one appeared to be paying any extra attention to him.

The *Bowman* was crowded with passengers. No big gold strikes had been made in the Alaska Territory, but enough of the precious stuff had been found to make it attractive to those who hoped to get rich in a hurry. This was a new

generation of gold-seekers, Longarm thought as he stood at the ship's rail. They had been born way too late for the big Rush of '49, and almost twenty years had passed since the first discoveries of gold and silver in the Comstock Lode. Alaska was what was left, and these latter-day Argonauts were going to do their best to get their hands on a fortune before somebody else did.

Most of them were young, Longarm noted, though there were a few grizzled old-timers in search of one last strike among them. In fact, the two men who stood at the rail beside Longarm looked as if they would have been more at home on the campus of some college back East. Their clothes were good quality, but not the sort that would be very warm once they got where they were going, and the hands gripping the rail were soft. The eyes of the young men shone with excitement.

The one closest to Longarm turned to look at him and said, "This is going to be quite the adventure, isn't it?"

"I reckon so."

The young man put out his hand. "I'm Raymond Grantham." He was slender and of medium height, with brown hair and a thin but animated face.

"Custis Long," Longarm introduced himself. He didn't see any reason not to use his real name on this trip. Where he was going, there shouldn't be anybody who would know him.

"This is my friend Timothy Swain," Grantham said.

Longarm shook hands with him as well. Swain was a little taller than Grantham and more solidly built. There was a childlike anticipation on his face. Of the two, Longarm judged that Grantham was the more intelligent, but both of them struck him as being way out of their depth.

"We left Harvard to come out here," Swain said, confirming Longarm's guess that they were college boys. "Raymond and I are going to find a gold mine and be rich."

"Well, that's the plan, anyway," Grantham said with a smile. "Perhaps we've set our hopes too high, but a man's reach should exceed his grasp, eh, or what's a heaven for?"

Longarm nodded. "I reckon that Browning fella had it right, sure enough."

Grantham looked a little surprised that Longarm had recognized the source of the quote, but he didn't say anything. Longarm smiled to himself.

With billowing sails, the *Bowman* eased out into the harbor and then turned toward the Golden Gate. It slipped through the opening and into the Pacific Ocean, where the wind picked up even more. With the excitement of the departure over, many of the passengers went below. Grantham and Swain stayed on deck, clearly not wanting to miss a moment of the voyage.

In less than half an hour of riding the choppy waves, both young men were hanging their heads over the rail, no doubt wishing they could go ahead and die, just to get it over with.

Longarm had never cared for sailing ships, either. He was at home on the hurricane deck of a horse, but not out here in the middle of the ocean. Still, his stomach was pretty strong. He stood at the rail—a good distance away from the two young would-be prospectors—and smoked a cheroot. The wind whipped away the smoke and blew in a strong, salt smell.

He wondered if Harrison Dodge had been sick during the voyage to Alaska. It seemed pretty likely to Longarm. If the little fella had been a clerk in some Washington office for years, he'd probably never even been on a sailing ship before fleeing from San Francisco. Longarm found himself hoping that Dodge hadn't fallen overboard. He would hate to think that he was going all the way north to Alaska for nothing.

"North to Alaska," Longarm muttered to himself. It had a good sound to it, but it was still a trip he wished he didn't have to make.

Chapter 4

The sun was brilliant in the blue sky overhead, but the wind that filled the sails and blew the ship on toward the rugged green coastline was chilly. Longarm turned up the collar of the sheepskin jacket and was glad he had bought the garment back in San Francisco. He shifted an unlit cheroot to the other side of his mouth and chewed on it some more as the *Bowman* approached the small port settlement of St. Michael, Alaska Territory.

Three weeks had passed since the ship had left San Francisco, and in that time it had made a broad loop out into the northern Pacific, skirting the gray and windswept Aleutian Islands. The ship had passed within sight of those islands, and Longarm had wondered at the time why anybody would want such bare, Godforsaken chunks of rock. The inhabitants were mostly Indians, he'd been told by one of the members of the *Bowman*'s crew, and they made their living by fishing. It wasn't any sort of living Longarm would want for himself, but he supposed it was all the Aleuts knew.

Once the islands had been circumnavigated, the ship had swung back to the northeast into the Bering Sea, heading for the Alaskan coast. Now the mainland was finally in sight. The shore was lined with low bluffs, and the waves crashed whitely against the rocks at the base of those bluffs. A coastal plain that seemed to be covered with scrubby trees stretched

inland, and beyond it ranges of low hills rose, also thickly wooded. From here, Longarm couldn't see any mountains, but he knew they were there, lurking snow-capped in the distance.

"It's quite pretty in its own stark fashion, isn't it?" Raymond Grantham asked as he came up to stand at the rail beside Longarm.

Longarm looked over and saw that Timothy Swain was with Grantham, as usual. He wasn't sure if he had ever seen the two of them apart. They were probably scared, even though they wouldn't want to admit it. This was quite an undertaking for a couple of wet-behind-the-ears Eastern greenhorns like them.

"I hear tell Alaska's a right pretty place—about three months out of the year," Longarm said with a nod of agreement. "The rest of the time it's covered with ice and snow and cold enough to freeze off a witch's tit."

Just that reference was enough to make the young and inexperienced Grantham blush. "I hope we can make our fortune and return to civilization before the weather gets bad again," he said.

"If this is summer, I'd hate to be here in the winter," Swain added. He had his thin coat pulled tight around him, but he was still shivering a little from the chill in the air.

Longarm hoped it wouldn't be quite so cold inland. For one thing, the wind wouldn't be blowing as hard. That would help.

Over the past weeks, he had grown friendly with Grantham and Swain, once they got over being as sick as dogs. Even though he hadn't told them that he was a lawman, really hadn't told them much of anything about himself, they seemed to look up to him, taking him for the sort of rugged Westerner they wanted to emulate. He didn't try to disabuse them of the notion, figuring it would just be a waste of time. So as the ship approached St. Michael through Norton Sound, he wasn't surprised when Grantham asked, "Would you consider perhaps partnering with us, Mr. Long? We could certainly use your experience."

"You fellas know just as much about Alaska as I do," Longarm replied, not quite honestly. He was a far cry from being an expert on the place, but it was a frontier, same as the ones farther south with which he was familiar. His years as a lawman had taught him a lot about surviving on any frontier, no matter where it was.

"Well, if you change your mind, we'd certainly love to have you travel with us," Grantham said.

Longarm nodded and said, "I'll keep it in mind," knowing he was going to do no such thing. He didn't want to be saddled with a couple of tenderfeet like Grantham and Swain, and besides, with any luck he would find Harrison Dodge at St. Michael and take him into custody right away. If that happened, the two of them would be on the next boat south.

The rest of the Argonauts lined the ship's railing as the *Bowman* sailed into the harbor, where one of the branches of the Yukon River emptied into the sea. St. Michael consisted of a handful of streets lined with log buildings, tents, and even a few tarpaper shacks. A couple of sturdy docks extended into the harbor, but no other ships were anchored there. A smaller wharf was located on the Yukon's estuary, about a quarter-mile inland on the other edge of the settlement, and Longarm spotted the tall smokestack of a steamboat that was tied up there. The mouth of the river was several hundred yards wide, and this wasn't even the main branch of the Yukon.

Longarm's teeth clenched on the cheroot as he bent to pick up the war bag and the Winchester at his feet. He was ready to have his feet on solid ground again.

The crew of the *Bowman* expertly dropped the sails, and a couple of ropes were tossed ashore to men who were waiting on the dock. They hauled hard, then snubbed the thick ropes around the pilings along the dock. Several crewmen jumped down from the deck to help make the vessel fast.

The would-be prospectors, carrying their gear, clustered around the spot where the gangplank would be extended to the dock. Like Longarm, they were impatient to be ashore,

but their reasons were different. They couldn't wait to start making their fortunes.

Most of them would return home broke and beaten, Longarm knew. That was the way of things when it came to gold hunting.

Raymond Grantham extended a hand to him. "Good-bye, Mr. Long. Thank you for your company on the voyage."

Longarm shook the young man's hand. "Good luck."

"And to you, too, sir."

Swain shook hands with Longarm, as well, and grinned as he said, "Next time you see us, Mr. Long, we're going to be rich."

"I hope you are, old son," Longarm said, and meant it. If the two youngsters were lucky, they would make a strike in a hurry and go home before the wilderness had a chance to gobble them up.

When his turn came, he slung his war bag over his shoulder, tucked the rifle under his arm, and went down the gangplank to the dock. He walked out onto the dirt street, which was still a little muddy from the spring snow-melt, and as always after a sea voyage it felt a mite strange that the earth was not moving under his feet. He adjusted to it quickly, however, and was pretty much himself as he strode down the street toward the nearest saloon.

It wasn't so much that he wanted a drink—although that was certainly true—but saloons were usually the best sources of information in frontier settlements. He didn't want to waste any time getting on the trail of Harrison Dodge.

The closest drinking establishment was a log building with a tin sign nailed over its door that read HANRATTY'S SALOON. Longarm stepped up onto the porch, which was littered with strung-up animal pelts, opened the door, and went inside. He found himself in a big room that extended the width of the building. Each side wall had a fireplace built into it. The bar was along the back wall. Crude tables and rough-hewn chairs filled up the space between the door and the bar. About half of them were filled with men drinking, and another dozen or so men stood at the bar. Longarm recognized quite a few of

them from the ship. As eager as they were, they had postponed their quest for gold in order to throw a few slugs of
who-hit-John past their tonsils.

Longarm made his way through the tables and found an
open spot at the bar. He knew the chances of finding any
Maryland rye in a place like this were slim, so he didn't
bother asking the bartender who came over to see what he
wanted. He asked for whiskey instead, knowing he would
likely get some home-brewed panther piss laced with gunpowder, but he figured he could tolerate it if it would help
him get the information he needed.

The bartender was a short, burly man with a bald head
and handlebar mustache that curled on the ends. He wore a
gray apron that had once been white over a flannel shirt. The
muscles of his arms and shoulders bulged the fabric of the
shirt.

"There you go," he said as he set a glass in front of Longarm. "Four bits."

"A mite steep on the price, ain't you, old son?" Longarm
commented as he dug coins from his pocket and dropped
them onto the bar.

The bartender shrugged his massive shoulders. "That's the
goin' rate around here, sport."

Longarm pegged the man's accent as coming from New
York City. He had been there before and hadn't cared for it.
Of course, that was probably because folks were trying to
kill him at the time, but he tried not to let things like that
color his thinking. He picked up the drink and tossed back
the whiskey, then grunted in surprise as he realized it wasn't
as bad as he had expected it to be.

The bartender smiled at him. "You see, it didn't poison
you after all."

"Nope, it didn't," Longarm admitted.

"Want another?"

"Sure." Longarm waited while the bartender took a bottle
and splashed more whiskey into the glass, then he said, "Selling drinks this good, I reckon you must get most of the traffic
around here."

The bartender shrugged again. "I do my share of business." He put his hand across the bar. "Name's Grover Hanratty."

Longarm shook the big, strong hand. "Pleased to meet you, Mr. Hanratty. Custis Long is my handle."

"Come up here looking for gold, did you, Mr. Long?"

"That's right," Longarm said. He sipped the whiskey this time, now that he knew it wasn't so vile it would rot the inside of his mouth if he didn't drink it quickly. "I'm supposed to meet up with a partner of mine, fella name of Dodge. Maybe you know him?"

Grover Hanratty frowned in thought. "Can't say as I do. What's he look like?"

"About this tall," Longarm said, holding out a hand. "A mite on the scrawny side, but he's tougher than he looks." That was the truth, he thought, remembering the way Dodge had clouted him in that hotel corridor.

Hanratty shook his head. "No, I'm afraid I don't know him. But you can ask around. Most everybody comes through here sooner or later."

"I'll do that," Longarm told him. "You got any law in this town?"

Hanratty's dark eyes narrowed suspiciously. "Why do you ask?"

"I just thought if there's a sheriff or a constable, he might know Dodge."

"Oh." Hanratty shook his head again. "No, there's no regular law. There's a territorial marshal all the way down at Sitka, the capital, but he doesn't get up here very often. We pretty much handle our own problems around here."

"Must make for trouble sometimes," Longarm said, making it sound like an idle comment. He drank some more of the whiskey.

"No, not too much. Up the Yukon, now, there's some wild country and wilder men. There's a gang of pirates up there that sometimes jumps the riverboats."

That reminded Longarm of something else that puzzled him. "I saw a riverboat tied up on the other side of town. I

didn't know there were any of them up here."

Hanratty nodded. "Sure, there are two or three sternwheelers that make the passage regularly up and down the river from Circle City. Men have been finding gold around there. Cap'n Asa Ridgway was the first one to take a steamboat up the Yukon." The mustachioed saloonkeeper sighed. "Poor old Asa passed away not long ago. Coughed his lungs out from the consumption."

Longarm grimaced and said, "Bad way to go."

"Well, there's not really a good way, is there?" Hanratty gestured toward Longarm's empty glass. "Want another?"

Longarm shook his head. It was pleasant here in the saloon. Small fires in both fireplaces kept the chill out of the air, and the whiskey was good. But he couldn't while away his time here, not while Harrison Dodge was still out there on the loose somewhere. Longarm figured he'd better pay visits to some of the other saloons in the settlement, hoping to pick up a lead to the fugitive.

"No, thanks, I'd better—"

"Hold on," Hanratty said suddenly. Angry voices came from down the bar. "I have to tend to this."

Longarm turned to watch as Hanratty headed toward the disturbance. He saw that three men were surrounding a fourth one, laughing and cursing him and shoving him back and forth. The fourth man was the smallest and oldest of the group. He had bushy white whiskers and a shapeless felt hat crammed down on his head.

The old man's three tormentors were all gold seekers off the *Bowman*, Longarm realized. He remembered seeing the men on the ship during the voyage from San Francisco but didn't know them beyond that.

"Here now!" Hanratty said in a loud voice. "What the devil's going on?"

One of the men grabbed the collar of the old-timer's dirty jacket. "This son of a bitch tried to steal our gear!" he accused.

"I never done no such thing," the old man protested. "I

just asked these fellers if they'd like to buy a map to a gold mine."

One of the other men said, "And while we were looking at his phony map, he tried to sneak off with our packs."

"That's a damned lie. The strap on one o' them packs got hung on my foot, that's all."

Hanratty held out his hand and ordered, "Let me see the map."

The three Argonauts looked at one another, then the one who held a creased and greasy piece of paper shrugged and handed it across the bar to Hanratty. "Sure, why not?"

Hanratty just glanced at it, then said, "Muleshoe, I've told you about trying to peddle these maps in my saloon. There's no gold in these places you've marked."

"How do you know that?" challenged the old man called Muleshoe. "You been up there to have a look-see?"

"No, but I've heard plenty from men who have and came back with empty pokes."

The man who had hold of Muleshoe's collar said, "So you mean he's a fraud as well as a thief? The old man ought to be strung up!"

Hanratty shook his head and gestured curtly. "Let go of him. He's just a harmless old fool."

Muleshoe jerked against the hand that held him. "Fool, am I? One o' these days, I'll show you who's a fool! I'll be the richest man in the whole damn territory!"

The man holding him shook him roughly. "Shut up! We're going to teach you a lesson, old man."

"I said to turn him loose," Hanratty warned from the other side of the bar.

"Keep your nose out of it, mister. This is between us and the old coot."

With that, the man holding Muleshoe suddenly sank his other fist in the old man's belly. The brutal punch made Muleshoe gasp in pain and try to double over. He couldn't because of the grip on his collar holding him upright.

"Damn it!" Hanratty cried. He reached under the bar and came up with a bungstarter.

Before he could swing it, though, one of the other prospectors drew a pistol and slashed the barrel across Hanratty's face, opening a gash in his forehead. Hanratty stumbled back against the wall, pawing at the blood that gushed down into his eyes from the wound. The man who had pistol-whipped him lifted the gun, clearly intending to start taking some potshots at the bottles of liquor lined up along the back bar.

Longarm palmed out his Colt as he took two fast strides that brought him within reach of the gunman. He reversed the revolver and chopped the handle of it into the back of the man's head. The man's knees folded and the gun in his hand slipped from suddenly nerveless fingers to thud onto the bar. Longarm shoved the falling man out of his way and spun the Colt on his finger so that the butt slapped back into his palm. He leveled the weapon at the man who was about to hit Muleshoe in the belly again.

"I wouldn't," Longarm said quietly.

The third man's hand edged toward a gun tucked behind his belt.

"And I wouldn't do that if I was you, neither," Longarm said to him. "If I have to, I'll shoot you first, then this other son of a bitch."

"This is none of your business," snarled the man holding Muleshoe's collar.

"No, I don't suppose it is," Longarm said. "But I've always had a bad habit of buttin' into things that ain't none of my business—especially when some fella's beating up a harmless old codger."

"I . . . I ain't harmless!" Muleshoe gasped. "Lemme at 'im! I'll tear 'im limb from limb!"

"Settle down, old-timer," Longarm said. "This fight's over."

From the other side of the bar, Grover Hanratty said, "It damned sure is." He had dropped the bungstarter and pulled a sawed-off greener from under the bar instead. As he brandished the double-barreled weapon, with blood still dripping down his face, he looked ready to blow anybody to Kingdom Come if they crossed him.

The man holding Muleshoe let go of him and shoved him away. "You had no call to butt in," he said to Longarm. "No call."

"Get out," Longarm said flatly. "And take this gent with you." He nudged the unconscious man with the toe of his boot.

The two men lifted their friend and half-carried, half-dragged him out of the saloon. The place had gone quiet when the fracas broke out, but as soon as Longarm holstered his gun and Hanratty replaced the sawed-off shotgun under the bar, the sound of voices and laughter came back.

Longarm turned to Hanratty, who was wiping blood off his face with his apron. "Sorry if I shouldn't have taken cards in that hand."

"Hell, don't be," Hanratty said. "I appreciate the help. Most folks around here know not to start trouble in here, but those boys were just off the boat."

"Same as me," Longarm pointed out.

Hanratty regarded him intently for a moment, then said, "I don't think you've been just off the boat anywhere for quite a while, Mr. Long."

Longarm grinned. "And I could return the compliment, Mr. Hanratty."

Muleshoe said, "How's about somebody returnin' my map, less'n one o' you fellers wants to buy it."

Hanratty shoved the paper at the old man. "Here. Get out, Muleshoe."

Muleshoe sniffed. "I might take offense at that there tone o' yours, Hanratty."

"Take offense all you want, just take it somewhere else."

Carefully, Muleshoe folded the map and tucked it away inside his ragged jacket. Then he squared his shoulders, lifted his head, and marched out of the saloon, his dignity intact.

Longarm inclined his head toward the door where Muleshoe had just departed. "Reckon that's a real map the old man's got?"

"No," Hanratty replied as he took a bar rag and dabbed at the blood still seeping from the cut on his forehead. "Mule-

shoe doesn't know anything about finding gold. He claims he was a Forty-niner and made a fortune in California during the Gold Rush, but I figure that's just a pack of lies he uses to cadge drinks from men who don't know any better. I've never seen him with a single nugget or a speck of dust that he didn't beg off of somebody."

"Still, you didn't want those fellas hurting him."

"Muleshoe's harmless as long as you're not gullible enough to believe anything he says. But that's no reason to get rough with him." Hanratty reached for a bottle. "Sure you don't want another drink? It's on the house. That's small enough payment considering that you probably kept the place from getting shot up."

Longarm shook his head. "I'm obliged, but I reckon not. I've got things to do."

"Men looking for gold always do. Good luck to you."

"Thanks."

"And keep your eyes open," Hanratty advised as Longarm turned toward the door of the saloon. "I don't think those three gents have the backbone to jump you again, but you never know."

"I'm in the habit of watching my back trail," Longarm told him.

Hanratty nodded. "I figured as much."

"Can I leave my war bag and rifle here while I take a look around town?"

"Sure," Hanratty agreed. "I'll put 'em behind the bar and keep an eye on them for you."

Longarm didn't see any sign of Muleshoe or the three men he'd tangled with as he stepped out of the saloon. He looked down the street, seeing several more saloons and a couple of general stores. He also studied each face he saw. It would be quite a coincidence if he ran into Harrison Dodge on the street, but it wasn't out of the realm of possibility.

However, he didn't see Dodge, either. He walked down the street, stopping for a drink in each of the saloons. He didn't find out anything except that Grover Hanratty had far and away the best booze in St. Michael. A visit to each of

the stores didn't turn up any leads to Dodge, either. Longarm used his story of meeting a partner here in the settlement before starting upriver. That lie was a double-edged sword, Longarm knew. It might lead him to Dodge, but if the fugitive was still in town and heard that someone was looking for him, he would likely take off like a scared rabbit. Dodge would know good and well that he wasn't supposed to rendezvous with anyone here.

The good thing about it was that St. Michael wasn't very big. If Dodge wasn't here, Longarm ought to be able to establish that pretty quickly, and then he could move on to the next step. Hanratty had said that there were steamboats heading up the Yukon to Circle City fairly regularly. It was possible that Dodge had taken passage on one of those boats. If that proved to be the case, Longarm had no choice except to keep on following him.

His long strides carried him toward the riverfront. The sternwheeler was still tied up there. He could check with the boat's captain, Longarm thought, and find out if anyone matching Dodge's description had traveled upriver to Circle City in the past week.

As Longarm walked along, he reflected on the fact that he hadn't seen a single, solitary woman here in St. Michael. That wasn't too surprising. Women were always in short supply on the frontier—any frontier—and that was one reason they were so highly prized. Alaska Territory was still in the early stages of development. Even with the lure of gold, unless there was a big strike that created another rush, it would be a while before the prostitutes and gamblers who always followed the gold seekers drifted north. There might be a couple of Indian squaws selling themselves in one of the tents or shacks—no solidly built blondes of the sort that Harrison Dodge preferred—but that was probably the extent of St. Michael's female population at the moment.

Those thoughts passing through his head just added to Longarm's surprise when he suddenly heard the high, clear

voice of a woman as he approached the riverboat. Even more surprising was what the woman was saying.

"Back off, you son of a bitch, or I swear I'll blow a hole clean through you!"

Chapter 5

"Damn it, Katie, put that scattergun down before somebody gets hurt!"

"I won't warn you again, McConnell! Back off! And it's Captain Ridgway to the likes of you!"

Longarm reached the wharf and stepped out onto it as he heard the angry voices shouting at each other. He saw a group of men on the rear deck of the sternwheeler, just in front of the large paddles. They weren't all men, however, he realized as he took a closer look at the figure backed up against the wall of the boat's cabin structure. Thick, dark hair tumbled around her shoulders, and high, firm breasts pushed out the front of the man's shirt the woman wore under a fringed, buckskin jacket. Whipcord trousers hugged swelling hips and strong-looking thighs. Definitely a woman.

But she held the sawed-off shotgun in her hands with the ease and familiarity of a man. As she pointed the weapon at the men crowding in toward her, the tense lines of her body indicated that she wouldn't hesitate to use the shotgun if she had to.

The wheels of Longarm's brain were turning over rapidly. Captain Ridgway, the woman had called herself. Grover Hanratty had said that a Captain Asa Ridgway was the first man to take a steamboat up the Yukon. But that Captain Ridgway was dead, according to Hanratty. The woman on

the boat was in her twenties. That made her Asa Ridgway's daughter, or less likely, his widow.

The man in the forefront of the group facing the shotgun-wielding woman said angrily, "Blast it, we told you we didn't want any trouble. We just offered you a business deal—"

"Outright thievery, that's what you offered!" the woman snapped.

Angry mutters came from the other men. The leader put out a hand to stop them as they started to surge forward. He was a tall, rangy man in denim trousers, a heavy blue canvas jacket, and a sailor's cap perched atop a rumpled thatch of red hair. "Take it easy, Katie—" he began.

The twin barrels of the sawed-off lifted. "I warned you about that!"

The redhead rubbed a knobby-knuckled hand over his lantern jaw. "All right," he said harshly. "Captain Ridgway, if that's the way you want it. We offered you a fair price for the boat—"

The woman interrupted him again. "Highway robbery!"

A short, thick-bodied man standing just behind the redhead said, "That's enough, Ben. Let's throw this damned hellcat into the river and get on with it." Again, murmurs of agreement came from the other men.

The redhead hesitated, glanced back at his companions, then looked at the woman again. He gave her a cocky grin. "You see how it is, Katie. You cooperate with us, or you'll wind up with nothing but a dunking in the Yukon."

The woman's lips pulled back from her teeth in a snarl. "Just try it!" she said. "I warn you, Ben McConnell—the first barrel of this shotgun goes right in your belly!"

McConnell paled a little at the threat, but his jaw clenched angrily. This confrontation had gone too far for anyone to back off now.

So Longarm figured it was a good time for him to step up onto the gangplank leading from the wharf to the deck of the riverboat and say, "Howdy."

The woman's eyes jerked toward him in surprise, and in that instant, Longarm realized he had misplayed his hand.

McConnell's arm swept out, his fingers closed around the barrels of the sawed-off, and he wrenched them skyward. The woman pulled the triggers, but it was too late. Both charges boomed harmlessly into the air.

"Get her!" one of the men yelled.

McConnell wasn't able to hold his companions back this time. They lunged at the woman, bulling past him. From their shouts, it was clear they intended to grab her and toss her into the river.

Longarm wasn't going to have the blame for that icy dunking on his head. For the second time in less than an hour, he pulled his Colt and stepped into a situation that was getting rapidly out of hand.

As a couple of the men grabbed the woman and she cried out in a mixture of fear and rage, Longarm fired over their heads. The blast of the gunshot made everyone freeze.

"You fellas better do like the lady said and back off," Longarm told the men as he lowered the barrel of the Colt so that it was pointing in the general direction of the group. "The next one won't go into the air."

McConnell glared at him. "Who in blazes are you?"

"Just an hombre who don't like the idea of a pretty woman being thrown in the river."

"Hell, he's some kind of cowboy," cried the burly man who had urged McConnell on. "We don't have to be afraid of him."

Longarm shifted his aim a little, so that he was staring coldly at the man over the Colt's sights. "You willin' to bet your life on that, old son?"

The man swallowed hard and suddenly didn't look nearly as confident. McConnell took advantage of the opportunity to seize control of the group again. "Back off!" he shouted, waving his arms at them. "Back off, damn it! Can't you see that long-legged bastard's crazy enough to gun us all down?"

Longarm let the "long-legged bastard" comment pass— this time. He nodded as he came on up the gangplank and stepped onto the deck of the riverboat. "Now you're being

smart," he said. "Let go of the lady and step back by that paddlewheel."

The woman jerked her arms out of the grip of the men holding her. She glowered at McConnell and his cronies as they slowly moved back, then switched her glare to Longarm. "I didn't need any help," she said.

Longarm reached up and tugged on the brim of his flat-crowned, snuff-brown Stetson. "Then I'm beggin' your pardon, ma'am," he said. "Reckon I must've misread the situation." He started to lower the Colt.

"Wait a minute!" the woman said hurriedly. She reached into the pocket of her buckskin jacket, brought out a couple of shotgun shells, and broke open the sawed-off to reload it. Once she had dumped the empty shells and stuffed the fresh ones into the barrels, she snapped the weapon closed and said, "Now I can handle this worthless pack of scum."

"How dare you call us that?" McConnell said. "We never gave your pa a bit of trouble! We were a fine, loyal crew to Cap'n Asa."

The statement confirmed that the woman was Captain Asa Ridgway's daughter, Longarm thought. And from everything he had heard, he was able to guess that the captain's daughter was trying to carry on in his place, following his death. Evidently the crew of the riverboat hadn't been too pleased with that arrangement, however.

"You call yourselves loyal?" the woman scoffed. "Is this how you honor my father's memory, by trying to steal his boat?"

"We're not stealing it," McConnell raged. "I'll say again, we offered you a fair price. We even offered to let you keep a share of the profits."

"The profits from *my* boat!"

McConnell ignored her. "But we're not going to crew for you, Katie. Not for you, nor any other woman."

"Why, I've forgotten more about riverboats, and about the Yukon, than you'll ever know, Ben McConnell! And don't call me Katie!"

McConnell shook his head and said, "It doesn't matter. We won't work for you."

So this was a labor dispute, Longarm thought. He figured it was safe now to put his gun away, since the woman had reloaded her shotgun and once again had it menacing the group of angry men, so he slid the Colt back into the holster on his left hip.

"If you won't work for me," the woman said, "then get the hell off my boat!"

McConnell stared at her. "What are you saying?"

"I'm saying that you're fired, each and every one of you worthless oafs! Get off! Get off before I shoot you all for trespassing!"

Longarm heard a quaver in the woman's voice that told him she was dangerously close to hysterics. McConnell must have heard it, too, and realized that in this condition, she might actually pull the triggers and send that double load of buckshot tearing into him and the other men at close range. He gestured curtly toward the gangplank and said, "Come on, boys."

"You mean we're givin' up, just like that?" The question came from the short, burly man who had egged McConnell on earlier. "That ain't right, Ben. By all rights, this should be our boat."

"Cap'n Asa left it to *her*," McConnell said, disdain clearly sounding in his voice. "There's no point in arguing with a *woman*."

"Especially one with a sawed-off shotgun pointing at your belly," the woman said, her lip curling with some scorn of her own.

Longarm moved aside so that the men could file off the boat and down the gangplank to the wharf. He kept his hand ready to reach for the Colt again, just in case. The woman covered the men with the scattergun as they left the boat. McConnell was the last one off. He looked at her and said, "You haven't heard the last of this, Katie."

"Go on," she said. *"Git!"*

McConnell turned and stomped down the gangplank, the

stiff lines of his back revealing just how furious he was.

The men went down the street in a straggling line, past the curious onlookers who had been drawn to the vicinity of the wharf by the double-barreled blast of the sawed-off and the sharper crack of Longarm's six-gun. A few of the bystanders laughed, which just increased the foul mood of the riverboat's former crew.

When they were safely gone, the woman turned to Longarm and blazed, "What the hell did you think you were doing, mister? You could've gotten me thrown in the river."

"Not hardly," Longarm said. "They'd have had to throw me in first."

The woman lowered the shotgun and tucked it under her arm. "Spare me the chivalric boasting. Do you always go around butting in where you're not wanted?"

Longarm thought about what had happened in Hanratty's Saloon and grinned. "Seems to be a habit of mine," he said.

"Well, you can forget about it where I'm concerned. Captain Kate Ridgway doesn't need any help from anybody."

"That'd be you," Longarm said. "Daughter of Captain Asa Ridgway."

For the first time, the woman looked more curious than angry. "That's right. Did you know my father?"

"No, but I heard of him. Grover Hanratty said Asa Ridgway was the first man to take a steamboat up the Yukon."

Kate Ridgway's expression softened slightly at the mention of Hanratty. "Grover and my father were friends. And he's right. The *Yukon Queen* was the first steamboat up the Yukon."

"This vessel?"

Kate nodded. "Yes. And she's still the best boat on the river."

"But without a crew."

Kate's face hardened again. "What business is it of yours?"

Longarm held up his hands in self-defense. "Not a bit, only I might be looking for a way to get upriver to Circle City myself."

"Oh," Kate said, with the air of a woman who has just figured out the answers to all the questions. "So you're a prospector."

Longarm nodded. "Came up here to meet my partner and make our fortune."

"Where is he?"

"Don't know. Maybe you've seen him?" Longarm recited Harrison Dodge's description yet again, then said, "Could be he's already gone up to Circle City."

Kate shook her head. "Not on the *Yukon Queen*, he hasn't," she said. "I've seen every passenger we've carried, and that fellow wasn't one of them."

"What about one of the other boats? Could he have traveled on one of them?"

She shrugged. "I couldn't say. You can ask next time one of them comes into town."

That was exactly what Longarm intended to do if he didn't find Dodge before then. He said, "By the way, my name's Custis Long."

"You know who I am already," Kate said. "I'd say that I'm pleased to meet you, Mr. Long, but that would be a lie."

He grinned at her. "Mighty plainspoken, aren't you, ma'am?"

"Being honest is one of the many things my father taught me."

"And skippering a riverboat is another?"

"That's right," she said, giving him a defiant stare. "Do you have a problem with that, too?"

"No, ma'am, not at all. I'd say that McConnell fella and the rest of those men do, though."

For a second, Kate Ridgway looked tired and on the brink of despair. Then she stiffened her back and squared her shoulders and said, "Those men are fools. I don't need them."

"You can't operate a riverboat by yourself," Longarm pointed out.

"I won't have to. I'll just hire another crew. If you want to book passage to Circle City, you just come back in a day or so. The *Yukon Queen* will be ready to go."

"Yes, ma'am," Longarm said, though he had no idea if her prediction would prove to be accurate or not. He tugged again on the brim of his hat and turned toward the gangplank.

"I mean it," Kate said to his back. "I'm not going to give up just because of a bunch of stupid . . . stupid . . . oh!"

Longarm left her there searching for the proper word to express her disgust with Ben McConnell and his companions. He had no idea whether Kate Ridgway was a good riverboat captain or not.

But with that voluptuous figure of hers, and that heart-shaped face, and those deep brown eyes, she was surely one of the *prettiest* riverboat captains he had run across in a month of Sundays.

While he was talking to Kate, Longarm had watched from the corner of his eye as Ben McConnell and the other members of the mutinous riverboat crew entered one of the saloons. He headed that way now and, seeing that the saloon had a side door opening into the alley beside it, slipped into the place through that door. He found himself in an alcove where a poker game was going on. The men at the table didn't even look up from their cards as Longarm slouched past them.

McConnell and the other men were standing at the bar, talking among themselves in loud, angry voices as they threw down drinks. Longarm leaned a shoulder against the side of the arched entrance leading from the saloon's main room into the alcove. McConnell and the others weren't looking in his direction, so he was able to listen to them without them knowing he was there.

"—tell you, that she-devil will never be able to get another crew," McConnell was saying. "Put the word out, Carpen. Any man who joins the crew of the *Yukon Queen* will answer to me!" McConnell smacked his big right fist into the palm of his left hand to punctuate the threat.

His burly lieutenant, who was evidently named Carpen, nodded. "Sure, Ben," he said. "You just watch. In a few days

that bitch will come crawlin' back to us, beggin' us to let her take our offer!"

McConnell drained the last of his beer and thumped the empty mug down onto the bar. He dragged the back of his other hand across his mouth and said, "Damn right she will."

Longarm frowned. If Kate Ridgway wanted to captain the riverboat herself, she was well within her rights to do so. She had inherited it from her father and could do with it whatever she chose. But she had to have a crew if she wanted to continue making the run up to Circle City, and clearly, McConnell was going to try to prevent that from happening.

For all Longarm knew, Kate might be a terrible captain. But he didn't like the idea that McConnell was scheming to prevent her from even having an opportunity to succeed.

Still, it was really none of his business, he reminded himself. He was here to find Harrison Dodge, not to get mixed up in the trouble between Kate and her former crew.

A quiet step and a soft touch on his arm made him look over. To his great surprise, he found himself looking at another white woman, and damned if she wasn't a short, lushly-figured blond of the sort that Dodge apparently couldn't resist.

"Hello, there," the woman said. "Buy a girl a drink?"

Despite his surprise, Longarm grinned at the time-honored come-on. "Why, howdy, ma'am," he said. "I reckon I could do that, only . . . have you got some place more private than this where we could both have a drink?"

She returned his grin. "My, you don't waste any time, do you? You must be a man who knows what he wants."

That was true enough, though right now what he wanted probably wasn't exactly what she thought he had in mind. He wanted to ask her about Harrison Dodge, and he wanted to do it someplace where he wouldn't be seen by Ben McConnell and the other men from the *Yukon Queen*. They probably wouldn't take kindly to his presence right about now, and he didn't want his visit to this saloon to wind up in a brawl.

Longarm slipped a coin from his pocket and pressed it

into the blond's palm. "Why don't you just get us a bottle of the best stuff in the house and tell me where to meet you?"

"Honey, *I'm* the best stuff in the house—but I know what you mean." She leaned closer to him. "Go around back. There's some lean-tos there. I'll meet you in a couple of minutes."

Longarm nodded. "I'll sure be there."

He faded back through the alcove while the blond headed toward the bar. The poker players still didn't look up as he left.

There were three lean-tos along the back of the building, all made of logs and fairly sturdy. Longarm waited next to them, smoking a cheroot, and after a few minutes, the woman came around the corner of the saloon, clutching a shawl around her shoulders with one hand while in the other she skillfully carried a bottle and two glasses.

"This one here in the center is mine," she said. She went to the plank door and told Longarm, "Pull the latch string, will you?"

He opened the door and stepped back to let her go in first. As he followed, he had to stoop in order for his head to clear the top of the door. The slanting ceiling inside was high enough for him to stand upright, but just barely.

"I know it doesn't look like much," the woman said, "but it's home." She set the bottle and glasses on top of a small barrel beside the narrow bed. The barrel, the bed, and a steamer trunk were the only items of furniture in the room. A lantern sat on the steamer trunk. The woman lit it, then pushed the door closed. Without the lantern, the tiny, windowless room would have been plunged into darkness.

She sat down on the bed, which was covered with a bearskin robe. She patted the robe beside her, indicating that Longarm should sit, then pulled the cork on the bottle and started pouring drinks.

Longarm hung his hat on the door latch, for want of a better place, then sat on the bed beside the blond. She handed him one of the glasses, which was half-full of amber liquid. "Here's to you, my friend," she said.

"And to you," Longarm replied as he lifted the glass and clinked it against hers.

"My, ain't you the sweet one." The blond tossed back the drink, then set the glass on the barrel again and reached over to take Longarm's free hand. She raised it to her breast. "You can take as long as you like with me, mister. We don't get many men as handsome as you around here."

Her breasts were large and plump and soft, and Longarm enjoyed the feel of the one he was squeezing through her dress. The dress itself was plain gray wool and buttoned up to the neck. It was too chilly in these parts for the sort of thin, short, frilled and spangled gowns that saloon girls usually wore.

Longarm finished the whiskey in his glass—not as good as Grover Hanratty's, but not terrible—and leaned past the blond to set the glass next to hers on the barrel. While he was in that position he went ahead and put his arms around her. She tilted her head back and closed her eyes, a gesture that struck Longarm as oddly demure but very appealing. He kissed her, tasting the whiskey on her mouth. The tip of his tongue teased her lips, and she opened them to let him in.

The kiss continued for a long moment, then she broke it and said raggedly, "My name . . . my name is Caroline. I like for gents to know it before they . . . before they . . ."

"Custis," he said. "That's my name. I'm mighty pleased to meet you, Miss Caroline."

She was probably close to thirty years old, but he had a feeling that she hadn't been a soiled dove for a long time. He wondered if she had come up here to Alaska with her husband to hunt for gold, and then something had happened to him. A woman in that situation would have a hard time of it if she didn't have enough money for her passage back home. She might easily turn to what Caroline was doing in order to survive.

She kissed him again, and he brought his hand up to cup her cheek. He made the kiss long and tender and didn't stop until she was clutching at him. The brazen prostitute she'd

58

been pretending to be earlier was gone now. In her place he found a truly willing, wanting woman.

Longarm wanted her, too. It had been a lengthy voyage from San Francisco with only memories of Glory to keep him warm. And he had found Kate Ridgway undeniably attractive, too, though unapproachable. Caroline was anything but. She had one hand on his crotch already, groping at his stiffening manhood.

"How . . . how do you want to do this?" she panted as he broke the kiss again.

"Whatever suits you, darlin'," he said.

"You get on the bottom. I want to ride you."

"Sounds good to me."

"First, though, we got to get rid of some of these clothes. . . ."

She stood up, tossed the shawl aside, and began unbuttoning the gray dress. A moment later she had it off, revealing that she wore only a shift underneath it. Her large, dark-brown nipples were plainly visible through the fabric of the shift, which ended high on her solid thighs.

"Let me get your boots," she said. She turned away from him, straddled one of his legs, and bent over to pick up his foot. From that angle, as the shift hiked up, he had a good view of the dark pink slit between her legs and the thick, sandy-blond thatch around it.

Longarm reached out and ran a fingertip along the fleshy folds. They were already quite damp with the juices seeping from her. She shivered at his touch. "That feels so good," she said as she grasped his boot and pulled it off. She switched to the other leg and took that boot off as well.

Meanwhile, Longarm took off his coat and shucked his gun belt. He coiled it around the holstered Colt and set it onto the hard-packed earthen floor beside the bunk, where the butt of the Colt would be within easy reach once he was lying down. He unbuttoned his shirt and took it off, then unfastened his trousers and lifted his hips to slide them down over his legs. Caroline helped him remove them.

That left him in his long underwear. His shaft was fully

erect now, bulging against the garment. Caroline eyed it and said, "Dear Lord. I've got to get a better look at that. Lie back, Custis."

He did so, and she pulled his underwear down so that his long, thick organ bobbed up free and proud. Caroline perched on the narrow bed beside him and put both hands around his shaft.

"I never saw such. I'm not sure it'll all fit in me, Custis—but I sure intend to find out. Before I do, though . . ."

She leaned over and took the head into her mouth, swirling her tongue around it and nipping lightly with her teeth at the opening. Longarm felt his whole shaft throb in pleasure and anticipation.

Caroline might be relatively new at this, but she had a natural talent for giving French lessons, Longarm decided. He came close to blasting his seed into her mouth before she finally lifted her head from his groin and pulled up her shift. She straddled his hips and grasped his pole to guide it into her as she lowered herself.

She was wrong: all of Longarm's shaft fit into her, but just barely. The tip of it was tickling the very depths of her sheath when she finally bottomed out. She closed her eyes and rested her palms on his broad, hairy chest. "Don't move," she said in a choked voice. "I just want to enjoy . . . being filled up . . . for a minute."

Longarm kept his hips still and didn't thrust up into her, but he stroked her thighs and then ran his hands over the rounded mound of her belly before reaching up to cup her breasts through the thin material of her shift. The warm, fleshy globes more than filled his palms. He kneaded and caressed them as she began to slowly pump her hips back and forth.

That pace gradually increased, and Longarm had no choice but to fall in with the rhythm Caroline established. His shaft slid wetly in and out of her. Her breath came faster and faster. Their lovemaking didn't have the intense, hurried urgency of some encounters, nor was it slow and languorous like others. Instead, it was a steady building and building of

passion until both of them reached a peak and crested it. As they did, Longarm moved his hands from her breasts to her hips, grasping them to steady her as he drove up into her. His climax gripped him, the seed racing up his shaft to burst from the tip in thick, scalding streamers. Caroline cried out as he pumped her full to overflowing.

Longarm moved his hands up her sides to her shoulders and pulled her down to him. Their mouths met again in shared sweetness. He wrapped his arms around her and held her tightly.

Far in the back of his brain, the part of him that was still a lawman reminded him that he'd brought Caroline back here to ask her about Harrison Dodge. Longarm hadn't forgotten about that. He'd just . . . postponed it.

Wherever Dodge was, he could wait a few more minutes for Longarm to catch up to him. Right now, Longarm had his arms full of warm, contented woman, and that was how he was going to stay for a while.

Chapter 6

Longarm poured whiskey in the glasses and handed one of them to Caroline. "I sure didn't expect to find a woman like you here in St. Michael," he told her.

They were sitting on the bed, still half-undressed but wrapped in the bearskin robe to ward off the chill. Caroline sipped her drink and asked, "A whore, you mean?"

"I mean a sweet, good-hearted woman like yourself, darlin'."

She leaned her blond head against his shoulder and laughed. "You're nothing but a danged old flatterer, Custis—but I'm not telling you to stop!" She snuggled closer to him. "I reckon I'm the only white woman in these parts except for Kate Ridgway, and she's so cold-blooded she don't hardly count as a woman. A couple of Indian gals use the other lean-tos."

"You must have a lot of beaus."

Caroline laughed again. "That's a mighty delicate way of putting it. But, yeah, I stay pretty busy, what with all the miners passing through here on their way to Circle City."

"Could be my partner paid a visit to you," Longarm said. "Short little fella by the name of Harrison Emerson Dodge. Sometimes he goes by Harry."

"When you say short, do you mean in stature or . . ." Car-

oline slipped her hand into his long underwear and wrapped her warm palm around his manhood.

Longarm chuckled. "I wouldn't know about that. We're partners, but we ain't *that* good of friends. Ol' Harrison stands about a head shorter than me, and there ain't much hair left on his head."

"Would he have come through here about a week ago?"

Longarm felt a quickening of his pulse that had nothing to do with the way Caroline was sliding her hand up and down his hardening shaft. "That's right."

"I think I remember him. He never told me his name. I didn't think that was very nice of him. But he was kind enough in other ways. He asked me what was the quickest way to get to Circle City."

Now the caresses were getting to him, but Longarm retained enough presence of mind to ask, "What did you tell him?"

"I said he should take a steamboat. I guess that's what he did, because I haven't seen him around since then."

"The *Yukon Queen*?"

"No, it wasn't here then." Caroline pushed down Longarm's underwear so that she could get to his organ without as much trouble. Her head dipped toward it. "But one of the other boats was leaving the next day."

Longarm leaned back against the wall and rested his hand on her head as she took his shaft into the warm, wet cavern of her mouth. By opening her lips wide, she was able to engulf several inches of it. She started sucking gently but insistently.

Once again fortune had smiled on him, Longarm thought as he closed his eyes. Harrison Dodge was running true to form. During the fugitive's brief time in St. Michael, he had sought out the only woman in the area who suited his needs and had even indicated to her where he was going.

With that knowledge now in his possession, Longarm was content to sit back and enjoy what Caroline was doing to him. Her head bobbed up and down in his lap as she sucked him. He felt his climax roaring toward him like a runaway

63

train and warned her that she might want to stop what she was doing unless she wanted a mouthful of his seed.

The renewed enthusiasm with which she slid her lips up and down his organ told him that was exactly what she wanted. She reached between his legs and cupped his balls, rolling them back and forth in the palm of her hand as if to hurry their milky product on its way up his shaft.

Longarm's climax suddenly broke over him. Caroline clamped her lips tight around his fleshy pole as it started to spurt hotly into her mouth. Her throat worked as she swallowed, taking every bit of what he had to give her. Lower down on his throbbing shaft, her other hand clenched. She waited until what seemed to be the last of his juices had erupted, then lifted her mouth from his organ and milked out a final drop of thick, creamy fluid. Her tongue shot out and lapped it up eagerly.

His chest rising and falling rapidly as he tried to catch his breath, Longarm sat there and stroked Caroline's head as she rested it in his lap. His softening shaft lay against her cheek. She nuzzled it in contentment.

"I sure am glad I saw you come into the saloon, Custis," she said quietly.

"So am I, darlin'," he said.

And thinking of what she had told him about Harrison Dodge, he meant that in more ways than one.

Like most saloon keepers, Grover Hanratty seemed to know a lot about what went on in his town, so that evening Longarm strolled back into the big log saloon. He figured that Hanratty would be able to tell him when the next steamboat was leaving for Circle City. The *Yukon Queen* was already in St. Michael, of course, and Kate Ridgway had assured him that she would be able to hire another crew, but after eavesdropping on the conversation between McConnell and Carpen in the other saloon, Longarm wasn't convinced that was true.

He was surprised to see Kate herself standing in front of the bar, her palms resting on the hardwood, as she talked to

Hanratty. The saloon keeper saw Longarm coming, and as Hanratty's eyes cut past her, Kate looked back over her shoulder at Longarm.

"Oh, it's you," she said.

"You're welcome," Longarm said dryly.

"What for? I didn't thank you for anything." Then understanding dawned in her eyes. "Oh, so you think I should be grateful that you horned in when Ben McConnell and like Carpen tried their little mutiny. Well, I'm not. If you hadn't gotten involved, I would have been able to talk some sense into their heads."

The situation hadn't looked that way to Longarm, but he wasn't going to waste time arguing with her. He asked instead, "You got that new crew lined up yet?"

Angry fire flashed in her eyes. "Damn it, what do you know about that?"

"About what?" Longarm asked. He thought he probably knew the answer.

Hanratty was the one who supplied it while Kate glared at Longarm. The saloon keeper said, "Kate's been telling me how she's having a little trouble finding men who are willing to crew for her. Seems like somebody's been spreading the word that it's not safe to work on the *Yukon Queen*."

"Who'd do a lowdown thing like that?" Longarm asked innocently.

"You know perfectly well who's to blame!" Kate practically spat at him.

"Considerin' the way we've been getting along, it wouldn't surprise me if you said it was my fault, ma'am."

Her glower didn't lessen any, but she said, "No, it's McConnell and Carpen. I know those two. Their pride's been hurt, and now they'll go to any lengths to get back at me."

"Well, I'm sorry if I brought any of that on, ma'am. I truly am," Longarm told her.

Finally, her anger seemed to ease slightly. She sighed and said, "I suppose it really isn't your fault. I guess I've been fooling myself. Maybe I . . . I'm just not cut out to be a riverboat captain."

Good Lord, thought Longarm, was she about to cry? Tough-as-nails Kate Ridgway?

Her back stiffened and she said between clenched teeth, "But I'll never admit it to that no-good, redheaded son of a bitch McConnell."

Longarm relaxed. He wasn't sure he could have dealt with a weepy Kate Ridgway. An angry, profane one was more like it.

She turned an intent, narrow-eyed gaze on him and jerked her head toward an empty table. "Come sit down and have a drink with me," she said. Her voice carried a tone of command.

Longarm wasn't accustomed to taking orders from gals—or from anybody except Billy Vail, for that matter, and he didn't *always* do what Vail told him—but he supposed it wouldn't do any harm to go along with Kate. At least for the time being.

Grover Hanratty put a bottle and two glasses on the bar. "Here you go, you two," he said. When Longarm glanced at Hanratty, he thought he saw a twinkle of sorts in the man's eyes. Longarm suppressed the urge to snort in disbelief. If Hanratty thought he was going to play Cupid for Longarm and Kate Ridgway, the burly saloon keeper sure as hell had another think coming.

Longarm reached for a coin, but Kate said, "No, it's on me. I'm not broke—yet."

With a shrug, Longarm let her pay for the whiskey. It had been her idea, after all.

He picked up the bottle and the glasses, though, and carried them to the table Kate picked out. It was in a corner of the room, near one of the fireplaces, and the tables closest to it were empty, giving them a modicum of privacy.

They sat down. Longarm uncorked the bottle and poured the drinks, then slid Kate's glass over to her. She wasn't interested in drinking to anything. She picked up the glass and unceremoniously took a healthy slug from it.

"I can't believe I'm doing this," she said as she set the glass back on the table.

"What, having a drink with me?"

"No, that's bad enough. What I can't believe is that I'm about to ask you to go to work for me."

Longarm stared at her. The proposition had not taken him completely by surprise. On the way over here to the table, he had gotten an inkling of what Kate might say to him. But he still hadn't been convinced she would go through with it.

"I'm no riverboat man," he said.

"No, you're a prospector. But you want to get to Circle City, and the *Yukon Queen* is the fastest way for you to do that." She sighed. "I know you won't want to make the trip back downriver, so I won't even ask you. Maybe I can find some men who have gone bust up there looking for gold who'd be willing to sign on for the return trip."

"Why me?" Longarm asked.

"Well, for one thing, I know you're not afraid of Ben McConnell." Her brown eyes searched his face. "Or are you?"

So she was already desperate enough that she wasn't above appealing to his pride. She must have spent a long afternoon looking for new crew members.

"I don't know . . ." he began.

"Have you ever worked on a riverboat before?"

"I've done a lot of things," Longarm answered, truthfully but also noncommittally.

"I'll make it worth your while. You'll have to wait until we reach Circle City to get your pay, but I promise you'll have a good grubstake once you start looking for gold."

She was sincere. Despite what it had to be costing *her* pride, Longarm knew she meant every word she said.

And the idea wasn't a bad one, he told himself. Kate was right that the *Yukon Queen* was likely the fastest way for him to get to Circle City, where, if his luck continued, Harrison Dodge would be waiting for him. But there were still some obstacles in the way.

"Two people can't run a riverboat by themselves."

"No, they can't," Kate said. "We'll have to come up with the rest of the crew."

"We?" Longarm repeated.

"You'll be first mate," she declared. "That was Mc-Connell's job. One of your duties will be to help me recruit more crewmen. But that'll be easier once the men around here see that somebody is willing to defy McConnell."

She might be right about that. Anyway, Longarm decided abruptly, it was worth a try. His instincts told him to go along with this, and he had learned to trust his gut.

"Well, what about it?" Kate prodded. "Am I drinking with the new first mate of the *Yukon Queen* or not?"

"You are," Longarm said. He lifted his glass. "To the *Yukon Queen*."

"I'll drink to that," Kate said as she clinked her glass against his. "And to rubbing Ben McConnell's nose in it."

Kate Ridgway held her liquor just fine, Longarm discovered over the next hour. He didn't see any signs that she was drunk at all when she finally stood up from the table and said, "I've got to get back to the boat. Where are you staying?"

Longarm shrugged. "I haven't found a place yet. Hanratty's got my war bag and rifle stashed behind the bar for me."

"Get 'em and come on back to the boat. The first mate has his own cabin." She frowned at him. "But don't get any ideas."

"Nary a one, Cap'n, I promise. But how will it look if I spend the night on the boat like that?"

Kate laughed. "You think I've got a reputation left to protect? Not around here. Once I decided I was going to run the *Yukon Queen* myself, folks in these parts all decided I was shameless, anyway. Except for Grover, maybe."

Longarm got to his feet. "What about McConnell? Did he think being first mate carried some extra privileges with the job?"

"If he did, he learned soon enough that he was mistaken," Kate said crisply.

Longarm went to the bar and reclaimed his war bag and

Winchester from Hanratty, then said, "If you talk to anybody who wants to sign on with the *Yukon Queen*, send 'em on down to the boat."

Hanratty grinned. "I'll do that. So she got you, did she?"

"You're looking at the new first mate."

The saloon keeper laughed and said, "I figured as much. You treat that girl right now, Custis. She's not as hard-nosed as she takes on."

Longarm nodded. "Don't worry, Grover."

Hanratty became more serious as he said, "Keep an eye out for Ben McConnell. I've heard the talk going around about how he won't let anybody sign on with Kate. And watch out especially for Ike Carpen. McConnell's a hell of a bruiser, but he's direct about it. Carpen's the sly one."

"I'll keep that in mind."

With his bag slung over his shoulder and his Winchester tucked under his arm, Longarm went to the door to join Kate. They walked out of the saloon together and turned toward the riverfront.

As they strolled along through the chilly night, Longarm said, "If you don't mind my askin', how'd a gal like you come to want to run a riverboat?"

"What else am I going to do? It's my boat."

"I ain't disputin' that. Most folks of the female persuasion would rather do something else, though."

"Like sit around and sip tea and simper at some man? No, thanks. I've had my fill of that. Ever since my mother died when I was little, my father insisted that I go to finishing school in Seattle so that I could be a lady." Kate laughed. "It didn't take."

"Oh, I don't know. Just because you're the captain of a riverboat don't mean you can't be a lady, too."

"Well, you're the first man I've run into who has enough sense to see things that way. Ben never could."

"Seems to me that McConnell fella is a bit of a damned fool."

"He was fine starting out," Kate said, her tone growing surprisingly wistful. "After my father passed away, I took the

Queen up and down the river several times with no trouble at all from the crew. But then they started resenting the fact that I'm a woman. Enough of them are old sailors so that they regard any woman on a boat as being bad luck."

"So McConnell decided it would be better if he ran things."

"That's right. He said he'd buy the boat from me, and he didn't want to understand when I said it wasn't for sale."

"Well, I reckon he's got the idea through his head now."

"But he won't like it," Kate said. "His pride will never let him admit that I was just as good a captain as he would be."

Longarm shrugged. "Let him get his own riverboat if he feels that way."

Kate stopped walking and gave him a funny look. She said, "You know, I wouldn't be a bit surprised if he did just that."

Neither would Longarm, now that he thought about it. If Kate continued taking the riverboat up and down the Yukon, she would likely have even more competition soon enough.

They walked on, and as they neared the wharf where the *Yukon Queen* was tied up, Kate stopped short again and caught hold of Longarm's sleeve. "I think I saw somebody moving around on the deck!" she hissed.

Longarm's keen eyes searched the deck but didn't see any sign of movement. "Are you sure?" he whispered.

"I'm positive! I wouldn't put it past that damned Carpen to try to burn the boat!"

Longarm noticed that she didn't accuse McConnell of being capable of such villainy. At the moment, he didn't care who was skulking around the riverboat. Whoever it was had to be up to no good.

He dropped his war bag at Kate's feet and said in a low voice, "Stay here. I'll check it out."

"The hell I will! That's my boat."

"Well, let me take a look first, anyway," he insisted. He held the Winchester in both hands, ready to lever a shell into the chamber, and started forward, moving stealthily.

He had reached the foot of the gangplank when Kate let out a startled cry behind him.

Longarm swung around and saw that someone had come up behind Kate and grabbed her, looping an arm around her throat and jerking her head back. Starlight glinted on the blade of the knife the man held against her throat.

Heavy footsteps sounded on the deck of the riverboat behind Longarm. A harsh voice ordered, "Don't move, you bastard! Do as you're told or Brant'll cut that bitch's throat, sure as shit."

Longarm stood there on the wharf, frozen by the threat to Kate's life. The voice that had spoken from the boat sounded familiar, but he hadn't recognized it right off.

It went on, "Not such a big man now, are you, when you're not hittin' somebody from behind?"

Now Longarm was able to place the voice. It belonged to the varmint who had tried to beat up the old man called Muleshoe in Hanratty's Saloon that afternoon. Longarm turned his head enough to see over his shoulder. Two figures loomed darkly on the deck of the riverboat. The third man had hold of Kate. So all three of the men he had run out of the saloon were here, and they had come seeking revenge.

"Brant's head still hurts from you cloutin' him," the spokesman went on. "I reckon he figures havin' a little fun with your gal while you watch would be a good way of payin' you back for that."

The man with his arm around Kate's neck lowered the hand holding the knife so that it was pressed against her right breast. He laughed and said, "Lemme bring her on board so's I can go ahead and rut with her, House."

"Hold your horses," the spokesman ordered. "I want this bastard to put down his guns 'fore we do anything else."

Kate managed to choke some words past the arm that was pressed across her throat like an iron bar. "Custis . . . don't do it . . ."

"You hush, bitch!" Brant said as he jerked back even harder on Kate's throat. "Better be careful or I'll stick this knife up you 'stead of my dick."

Longarm breathed slowly and deeply, taking care to keep a tight rein on his emotions. The glance over his shoulder had told him that the two men on the boat had guns drawn. But the voices of both Brant and House were blurred by drink. They had probably been getting liquored up all day, working up the courage to strike back at him. He wasn't sure how they had known to set this trap for him at the *Yukon Queen*, but that didn't matter. One of them could have seen him and Kate leaving Hanratty's together and run on ahead to alert the others. He and Kate hadn't been in any hurry to reach the boat and had walked slowly while they were talking.

The whiskey he'd consumed at Hanratty's hadn't muddled him any. His mind was clear as a bell. He knew he could spin around with the Winchester in his hand and probably take the two men on the boat before they could drop him. But if he did that, Brant would have a free hand to carve up Kate with that knife. . . .

He was still turned toward Kate and Brant, so he saw the sudden movement as she jabbed behind her with her right hand. She grabbed something and twisted, and Brant let out a howl of pain.

Longarm let his instincts take over. He whirled toward the boat, dropping to one knee and levering the Winchester as he did so. Orange flame geysered from the barrel of one of the guns on the deck of the *Yukon Queen*, but the slug whipped through the air above Longarm's head. He fired the rifle from the hip, squeezing off three shots as fast as he could work the lever and jack fresh cartridges into the chamber, then kicked himself to the side. His shoulder landed on the rough planks of the wharf and he rolled over. A bullet chewed splinters from the boards just behind him. The muzzle flash gave him something to aim at as he sprawled out on his belly. He fired, levered the Winchester, fired again. Someone on the boat screamed.

Longarm thought he had scored on both of the bastards. He had to hope they were out of the fight, at least momentarily, because a few yards away, Kate was struggling des-

perately against Brant. She had managed to free her throat from his grip, but he still had hold of her with one hand and was trying to stab her with the knife in the other hand. She held on to that wrist with both hands.

Longarm surged to his feet and lunged toward the struggling figures. He couldn't risk a shot, not with Kate pressed up so tightly against her opponent. Instead he shouted, "Brant!" and when the man looked instinctively toward him, Longarm drove the butt of the rifle past Kate's shoulder and into his face. At the same time he crashed into both of them.

The collision knocked them apart and sent Kate falling to the ground as Brant staggered back several steps. Longarm saw the knife lying on the ground where Brant had dropped it. He kicked the knife away and leveled the Winchester at Brant, who stood holding his jaw and moaning.

"Give it up, old son," Longarm grated. "It's over."

"The hell it is!" Brant choked out thickly. He pawed at the pistol holstered on his hip.

Longarm shot him, the rifle bullet driving into Brant's chest and throwing him backward. Brant landed on his back in the loose-limbed sprawl that indicated death.

A rush of feet from behind came to Longarm's ears. He whipped around to see one of the other men rushing him, some sort of club held high, ready to dash out Longarm's brains. Before Longarm could fire, Kate reached in from the side and thumped her fist against the man's belly. He cried out, dropped his bludgeon, and clasped his hands to his stomach as his charge became a stumbling fall. He thudded to the ground a few feet from Longarm and rolled onto his side. Now Longarm could see the handle of Brant's knife protruding from the man's belly. Kate must have picked it up, and once it was in her hands, she knew what to do with it.

Longarm heard the death rattle in the man's throat. He stepped past the corpse and charged up the gangplank, searching for the third and final man. Longarm found him sitting on the deck of the riverboat, slumped against the cabin wall. The man's head was down, and a dark puddle of blood surrounded him. When Longarm prodded his shoulder with

73

the barrel of the Winchester, he toppled lifelessly to the side.

"Damn it!" Kate said from the wharf. "All that blood'll never come out of the deck boards."

Longarm looked at her. She had gotten to her feet and seemed to be fine. "Are you hurt?" he asked.

"No. After I nearly twisted his balls off, that son of a bitch wasn't nearly as enthusiastic about knifing me."

That wasn't exactly the way it had been, thought Longarm—Brant had still shown plenty of fight—but now wasn't the time to point that out. People were hurrying from the saloons toward the wharf, anxious to see what all the shooting and yelling had been about.

"Better get a lamp lit," he said. "It'll be awhile 'fore things settle down."

"Who were these men? They're not part of my old crew. McConnell didn't send them."

"Nope," Longarm said. "They were after me."

Kate grunted. "I'm starting to wonder if I made a mistake by hiring you, Long. But don't take that as an excuse to quit."

Longarm lowered the Winchester to his side. "Don't intend to."

But he wondered, too, if signing on with the *Yukon Queen* had been a mistake.

Chapter 7

By the next morning, the word had gotten around the settlement about the three men Longarm and Kate had killed. He had had a damned busy first day in St. Michael, Longarm reflected as he left Kate on board the riverboat and strolled down the street from the wharf where the *Yukon Queen* was tied up. Most of the men he passed looked at him from the corners of their eyes, as if both afraid and fascinated at the same time.

One thing was certain, though: the violence in which he had been forced to engage had given him some credibility in the eyes of St. Michael's inhabitants. Before, men might have been leery about signing on with Kate Ridgway because of Ben McConnell's threats. Now, with Longarm on board as the first mate, some would be less likely to worry about McConnell.

But it didn't completely negate the menace of McConnell's promised vengeance, however, as Longarm discovered over the next couple of hours. He went into Hanratty's Saloon intending to get some breakfast and sign up some crew members, but he accomplished only the first of those goals. Hanratty's Indian cook dished up a fine breakfast of caribou steaks, flapjacks, fried potatoes, and sourdough biscuits, along with a pot of strong, black coffee that Hanratty laced with brandy. But although some of the gold

seekers in the saloon asked Longarm about booking passage on the *Yukon Queen*, none of them were willing to work on the riverboat.

"Damn it, Grover," Longarm groused as he sat at the bar and sipped from another cup of the brandy-spiked coffee, "does McConnell cut such a wide swath that everybody in these parts is afraid of him?"

Hanratty put his palms on the bar and sighed. "Just about. He's been mixed up in brawls in every saloon from Fairbanks to Point Barrow, and he's come out on top in every one of 'em. Carpen and the rest of that bunch are just about as tough. The crew members of the *Yukon Queen* are famous for being men you don't want to cross. Former crew members, I should say."

Longarm drained the last of the coffee, took a cheroot from the pocket of his flannel shirt, and lit it with a lucifer. "You don't happen to want to sign up, do you, Grover?"

Hanratty laughed and shook his head. "I'm not afraid of McConnell or any of that bunch, but I've got a business to run here. I'm a saloon keeper, not a riverboat man."

Longarm took a drag on the cheroot and blew a smoke ring. "I ain't a riverboat man, either, but it looks like I'll have to be one for a while. I can't go back on my word to Kate."

"But the two of you can't handle that boat by yourselves, either."

"Nope. I—"

A tug on the sleeve of Longarm's sheepskin jacket interrupted whatever he'd been about to say. He looked over into the weathered, whiskery face of the old man called Muleshoe.

"I hear you're goin' up the Yukon," the old-timer said.

"That's right, but I ain't interested in buyin' no gold mine maps."

"What the hell makes you think I'd sell you a map? I'm gonna use it my ownself, once I get up there."

"Don't tell me you want to book passage on the *Yukon Queen*, too?"

Muleshoe shook his head. "Nope. Got no money to pay for a ticket. I want to sign on to work. I'll pay for my passage that way."

Longarm regarded the old man with narrowed eyes. Muleshoe was a scrawny little cuss, but that didn't mean he wasn't tough. Longarm asked, "You ever work on a riverboat before?"

"Just up an' down the mighty Mississip' from Cairo to New Orleans a hunnerd times or more," Muleshoe sneered. "That's all."

Hanratty leaned forward and said, "Are you sure about that, Muleshoe? I never heard you talk about working on the Mississippi. Lord knows you've talked about everything else."

Muleshoe bristled. "You callin' me a liar, Hanratty?"

"I'm saying you and the truth aren't very close acquaintances some of the time."

Muleshoe glared at him for a second, but didn't answer the question. He swung back toward Longarm instead and said, "Well, what's it gonna be, boy? You want an experienced hand for that boat or not?"

Longarm tried not to grin. "Maybe this just shows that I'm getting desperate, but . . . sure, why not?" He held out his hand. "Welcome aboard, Muleshoe. You got any other name?"

"Flynn," the old-timer said as he clasped Longarm's hand. "My real front handle's Maurice, but I'll carve the gizzard out'n any man who calls me that. Just make it Muleshoe Flynn."

"All right, that's what it'll be."

Hanratty shook his head. "I hope you're not making a mistake by taking on this old coot, Custis."

"Old coot, is it?" Muleshoe sputtered. " 'Least I ain't from New York City." He turned to Longarm again. "Hear you been havin' trouble signin' up fellas to work on that boat. I can put you onto a few who ain't a-scared o' Ben McConnell."

"That'd be just fine," Longarm said. "Do they have riverboat experience, too?"

"No, but beggars can't be choosers, now can they? Come on with me." Muleshoe jerked his head toward the door of the saloon.

Longarm glanced at Hanratty, grinned, and shrugged. He followed Muleshoe out of the saloon.

The old-timer led him to a crude shack on the edge of the settlement. It was a pretty unimpressive place. The thin door rattled on its leather hinges when Muleshoe pounded on it. "Come out o' there, you worthless old redskin!" he shouted.

A moment later, someone jerked the door open, and a fist came out in a wild swing. Muleshoe must have been expecting such a greeting, because he stepped back and let the punch go past him harmlessly. The man who had thrown it stumbled out of the shack, off-balance because of the missed blow.

Or maybe because he was drunk, Longarm thought. The shack's occupant was an Indian. That much was obvious from the ruddy skin, the high cheekbones, and the black hair that was worn in braids. This man wasn't as flat-faced as the native Alaskans, however. He wasn't an Aleut, a Tlingit, or an Eskimo.

Muleshoe jerked a thumb at the drunken man. "This here's Yak. He's called that 'cause he's a Yakima injun, from down on the Washington coast. He come up here 'cause o' some scrape he got into. He don't never talk 'bout it, but I figger he was messin' with some other buck's squaw."

Yak sneered at Muleshoe and said, "Noisy old man has face like porcupine's ass."

"Yeah, I'm right fond o' you, too, redskin." To Longarm, Muleshoe went on, "Yak's got three sons who live here with him, big ol' injun boys, hard workers. I reckon they're out fishin' now. That's how they get by and keep the old man in likker money. But all four of 'em will work on that riverboat for you and the gal. Ain't that right, Yak?"

The Indian drew himself up and stared solemnly, if blearily, at Longarm. "My sons and I will work on the *Yukon*

Queen," he said, as if he had been practicing the words. "You will pay us. We will work hard."

Longarm frowned and looked at Muleshoe. "I ain't too sure about this."

"Don't you worry none about Yak. Get him away from the hooch for a while and he'll be fine. And them boys of his are good boys. Just give 'em a chance, and you'll see."

"What about McConnell?"

Muleshoe cackled. "McConnell won't mess with the likes o' them. He won't think injuns is worth scarin'."

The old man might be right, Longarm thought. Besides, he had exhausted just about all his other possibilities. If he could come up with a crew, the riverboat would have a full load of passengers on its trip up the Yukon, and Kate would make enough money so that she could stay in business, at least for a while. It wasn't really his affair, of course, but the riverboat was still the quickest way to Circle City and Harrison Dodge. Besides, he had given Kate his word.

"All right," he said as he reached his decision. "But I want all the liquor out of that shack now."

Yak regarded him balefully. "No take hooch!"

"Then you don't get hired, old son." Longarm's voice was flat and hard, brooking no argument. "Get rid of the liquor, Muleshoe, and take Yak here down to Hanratty's. Pour coffee in him until he's sober. When will his boys be back from their fishing?"

"Prob'ly in 'nother hour or two."

"All right. Get them and Yak and bring them all to the *Yukon Queen* where you can keep an eye on them. I don't know when we're pulling out, but I'd like to get started as soon as possible. Sure wish I had a few more men, though."

"If I hear tell of anybody, I'll let you know."

Longarm nodded, hoping that any other prospective crew members Muleshoe came up with were in better shape than Yak. The Indian's sons might turn out to be all right, though, he reminded himself. The jury was still out on that question.

He left Muleshoe at Yak's cabin after reminding him about

getting rid of any liquor in the shack. As he walked back through St. Michael, Longarm studied the places he passed. He had already been through the saloons and stores this morning, searching for men who were willing to work on the riverboat, but his quest had been futile with the dubious exceptions of Muleshoe, Yak, and the Indian's sons. He was beginning to wonder if that would just have to be enough of a crew.

A groan came from an alley as he passed and caught his attention. He glanced down the narrow lane and saw a man sitting against the wall of one of the buildings, holding his head in his hands as he moaned in misery. Beside him, another man was lying on the cold ground, curled into a ball. Something about them struck Longarm as familiar, and as he paused he recognized them as the two youngsters from back East, Raymond Grantham and Timothy Swain.

Longarm walked into the alley. Grantham was the one sitting up. He lifted his head gingerly as he noticed Longarm looming over him. His eyes were bloodshot and red-rimmed. "M-Mr. Long?" he asked shakily.

Longarm hunkered on his heels, wrinkling his nose as he smelled the stench of vomit on the two young men. "What the hell happened to you boys?" he asked.

"I . . . I'm not sure," Grantham said. "We went into a saloon for a drink, and then these men asked us to play cards with them . . ."

Longarm rolled his eyes, then shook his head. "You two ever drink before?"

"We'd had some port and sherry, back at college . . ."

"I'm talking about real liquor."

"Well . . . no, I don't suppose so." Grantham winced and put his head in his hands again. His skull probably felt like it was cracking wide open, Longarm thought.

"Let me guess. You never played poker before, neither?"

"No, but it seemed like such a simple game."

"It wasn't the game that was simple, old son, it was you and your pard here."

Swain was either unconscious or sound asleep. His mouth

was open and breath rasped in and out of him to show that he was still alive. From time to time he shifted a little and grunted in pain.

"I guess we shouldn't have been so naive," Grantham said. "But it seemed . . . it all seemed like part of the adventure. Surely you understand, Mr. Long."

"Where's your gear?" Longarm asked.

Grantham's eyes widened, and he looked around frantically in the alley. "I . . . I don't see it! Where could it have gone?"

"How 'bout your grubstake?"

Grantham just looked confused.

"The money you and Swain brought with you," Longarm explained. "You still got it?"

Grantham reached inside his coat and then began slapping urgently at his pockets. "It's gone!" he announced as he looked up at Longarm in horror.

"Just like your gear." Longarm shook his head. "You won't ever see any of it again, I reckon."

"But without our gear and without any money, how will we reach the gold fields? How will we make our fortune?"

"I'd say that's the least of your worries right now. You got to figure out a way how to survive here in St. Michael until you can scrape up enough money to get back to the States."

Grantham covered his face with his hands. "Oh, God, no! We can't go back as failures, Mr. Long. We just can't!" He lowered his hands. "We boasted to everyone that we were going to be rich."

Longarm rubbed his jaw. He had an idea, but he didn't much like it. Still, the *Yukon Queen* could use a couple of extra hands. . . .

"You ever think about working on a riverboat?"

Grantham stared at him in confusion. "What?"

"I've signed on as first mate of a riverboat that's going up the Yukon to Circle City. That's in the middle of the gold fields. I reckon if you want to work your way up there, I can convince the captain to take you on, too."

Grantham reached out and clutched Longarm's sleeve. "You mean it, Mr. Long?" His voice trembled with renewed hope.

"There's just one problem. The fella who used to be first mate don't want anybody signing up to work on the *Yukon Queen*. There could be some trouble with him."

Grantham shook his head, then winced at the pain caused by that movement. "I don't care. Tim and I will risk it. We'll take any chance if it means we might still be rich."

Longarm thought that was pretty unlikely, but working on the riverboat would at least give the two youngsters a chance to get back on their feet again. They might not go home rich, but at least they would have had their chance.

"You can speak for Swain? He don't seem to be awake right now."

Grantham nodded. "Tim will go along with the idea, I'm sure. What do we have to do?"

Longarm wrinkled his nose again. "I ain't of a mind to share close quarters with a couple of fellas as ripe as you two. Let's get your pard on his feet and go find a bathhouse and laundry. Then we'll get some food and coffee in you."

"But . . . we don't have any money to pay for that."

"I'll stake you," Longarm said. "You can pay me back later." He didn't really care if he got the money back or not. It would all go on his expense account, and though Henry might bitch about it, Billy Vail would likely approve it. The important thing was staying on the trail of Harrison Dodge and catching up to the fugitive as soon as possible.

"Mr. Long, I . . . I don't know how to thank you."

Longarm stood up and extended his hand to Grantham. As he hauled the young man to his feet, he said, "Don't worry about it. This ain't no pleasure cruise you're going on. By the time we get to Circle City, you may not feel like thanking me."

The hot bath woke up Swain, but he and Grantham still felt mighty puny by the time Longarm herded them into Hanratty's like a pair of sheep. He had a hand on the shoulder

of each young man as he steered them toward the bar.

"These pilgrims need a surroundin'," he told Hanratty, "not to mention some black coffee."

"Two more reclamation projects, eh? At the rate I'm brewing pots of coffee today, I'm liable to run out of Arbuckle's." Hanratty grinned. "I reckon you want it straight, no brandy?"

Grantham and Swain both moaned at the mention of liquor.

"No brandy," Longarm confirmed. He looked around the room but didn't see Muleshoe and Yak. "You get that Indian I sent down here with Muleshoe sobered up?"

"Yeah, as much as I could. He's been putting away so much hooch he may have to sweat out the rest of it. Muleshoe said he'd take him on down to the boat." Hanratty put cups on the bar in front of Grantham and Swain and reached for the coffee pot sitting on the cast-iron stove. "Are you sure you know what you're doing, Custis? Hiring Muleshoe was one thing, but that Yakima . . ."

Longarm shrugged. "It don't look like I have much choice in the matter. I got to take the hands I can get."

Hanratty nodded and said, "I guess so. And old Yak's boys seem to be pretty steady. They might make good workers." He looked askance at Grantham and Swain, who were still pretty green around the gills. "Not so sure about these two."

Grantham swallowed and said, "We'll work hard for Mr. Long. You can count on that, sir."

"Sir, is it? Well, they're respectful children, anyway."

The two young men didn't want to eat, but Longarm insisted. The hot food hit their stomachs better than they expected, and a little color began to seep back into their faces. Longarm clapped them on the back and said, "That's more like it. You reckon you'll live after all?"

Grantham gave him a weak smile. "Maybe."

Around a mouthful of flapjacks, Swain said, "You know, this is actually pretty good."

When they had finished their meal, Longarm paid for the

food and coffee, then asked Hanratty, "You mind if I make an announcement?"

Hanratty waved a hand. "Go right ahead."

Longarm raised his voice and called, "Listen up, gents!" The murmur of conversation in the big room died away as the men at the tables turned to look at Longarm, who stood in front of the bar with his arms upraised. "The riverboat *Yukon Queen* will be leaving this afternoon, bound for the Yukon River and Circle City! We're now accepting passengers for the trip. To book passage, see me or Cap'n Ridgway at the boat."

"Cap'n Ridgway?" one of the gold seekers called out. "You mean that woman?"

Longarm fixed the man with a hard-eyed glare. "I mean the captain of the *Yukon Queen*. That's all you need to know, mister."

The man muttered something and looked down at the table where he was sitting. Longarm went on, "Come on, gents, plenty of room on the *Yukon Queen*! The fastest way to the gold fields!"

Another of the prospectors stood up and nodded. "I'll be down to book passage," he said. "You guarantee a fast run?"

"Fast as can be," Longarm promised.

"I'll be there," another man said, and yet another echoed him. Within moments, gold seekers all over the room were calling out their intention to book passage on the riverboat.

Grinning, Longarm looked at Hanratty and nodded. Then he said to Grantham and Swain, "Come on, you two. I reckon there's probably work to do before the boat can shove off."

He knew it wouldn't be long before Ben McConnell heard about the imminent departure of the *Yukon Queen*. The word would get around St. Michael in a hurry. That was one reason he had made such a public announcement. It was possible the boat could have slipped away from the settlement without McConnell noticing, but crawling away like a whipped dog had never been the way Longarm liked to do things. If

McConnell was going to make trouble, then by God let it come!

When Longarm, Grantham, and Swain reached the wharf where the sternwheeler was tied up, Longarm was surprised to see that three large, strapping young men were already carrying armloads of wood on board to fill the boat's fire boxes. They were unmistakably the sons of the Indian, Yak. Yak himself sat on a barrel on the boat's foredeck, looking glum but reasonably sober. Longarm asked him, "Where's Cap'n Ridgway and Muleshoe?"

Yak pointed with a thumb at the wheelhouse atop the boat's cabins. He didn't say anything.

Longarm turned toward the other Indians and said, "Howdy, fellas. My name's Long. I'm the first mate on this voyage."

They stopped toting wood long enough to shake hands with Longarm, who also introduced Grantham and Swain to their new fellow crew members. The two young men looked a little nervous about meeting up with a trio of Indians. Probably they had read too many dime novels in which Indians were either bloodthirsty savages or noble monarchs of the forest. This would be a good opportunity for them to learn that Indians were just folks like anybody else, some good, some bad.

In this case, they had white man's names: Joe, Pete, and Carl. They were all in their twenties, stolid, calm-faced men who carried themselves with an air of having seen just about everything the world had to offer and not being overly impressed by any of it. The oldest one, Joe, said to Longarm, "Thanks for the job, Mr. Long. We've been trying to figure out a way to get our pa out of this settlement. It's not good for him to be here."

Longarm nodded in understanding. "I'm glad you fellas signed on. I reckon once you finish filling the fireboxes, you better start stoking the boiler and getting some steam up. We'll be leaving later this afternoon, soon as we get a full load of passengers."

Longarm motioned for Grantham and Swain to follow him

as he climbed the ladder to the wheelhouse. The square, shacklike structure had large windows on three sides, giving the riverboat's pilot a good view of whatever waterway it was following. Longarm opened the door and stepped inside to see Kate Ridgway standing by the chart table, talking to Muleshoe. She didn't look happy.

When she turned to greet Longarm, she said sarcastically, "Couldn't you have found a more motley bunch?"

"Beggin' your pardon, little lady," Muleshoe said. "You got yourself the hardest-workin' crew on the Yukon." He looked at Grantham and Swain. " 'Cept for maybe these younkers. I don't know them. Maybe they's passengers."

"Nope," Longarm said with a smile. He waved a hand at the two young men. "This is Raymond Grantham and Timothy Swain, the last members of your crew, Cap'n."

Grantham and Swain stared at Kate. "She's mighty pretty," Swain said after a moment.

Kate took a step toward them, her brown eyes flashing with anger. "You won't think I'm so damned pretty when I get through with you! You two look too damned soft to work on a riverboat!"

Grantham and Swain flinched back from her lashing words. "I . . . I didn't mean any offense, ma'am," Swain said.

"And we don't mind working for a woman, ma'am," Grantham said. "Not at all, ma'am."

Longarm chuckled. "They're plenty wet behind the ears, but I reckon they'll be all right. Counting you and me, Cap'n, we've got a crew of nine. Is that enough?"

"Since Mr. Flynn tells me you weren't able to find anybody else, I suppose it'll have to be," Kate said. "We can manage with that number. Everyone will have to work hard, though."

"We're certainly willing to do that, ma'am," Grantham promised.

Kate turned to Longarm. "Men have already been by to book passage. They said you announced the boat was leaving this afternoon."

"Is that all right? Hope I didn't overstep my bounds."

She shook her head. "No, that's fine. Judging from the level of interest your announcement generated, I don't think we'll have any trouble selling all our available space by then."

"How many men can the boat carry?"

"We have eight cabins for passengers," Kate explained. "Usually three or four men are willing to share a cabin. We can put another twenty outside on the decks, but that's not as comfortable, of course. So between forty and fifty passengers is a good number for each trip."

Longarm nodded. "And they'll be showing up soon, I reckon." He turned to Grantham and Swain. "You boys go down and help load the passengers' gear."

"Yes, sir," the two young men said together. They left the wheelhouse.

"And as for you," Kate said, turning to Muleshoe, "I think you're going to be our new cook."

"Cook!" Muleshoe exclaimed. "Hell, I figgered I'd pilot the boat."

Kate smiled thinly. "I know the Yukon. You can go on down to the galley."

"But . . . but that's belowdecks!"

"If you'd rather stoke the boiler . . ."

Muleshoe held up his hands in surrender. "No, that's all right. I been coosie before. I reckon it won't hurt me to do the job again." He left the wheelhouse, muttering under his breath.

That left Kate and Longarm alone, and as she turned to face him again, he saw her struggling with her emotions. To head off her complaints, he said quickly, "I know it's not much of a crew, but they're the best I could find, like Muleshoe said. If we're lucky, we'll make out all right."

"I know that. It's just that . . ." She stepped closer to him. "I'm not angry, Custis, I'm really not. I'm just worried and . . . and excited at the same time. I was afraid the *Yukon Queen* had made its last trip with me in command."

He smiled at her. "Not hardly."

"And I've got you to thank for that."

"No, you don't have to thank—"

She startled him then by moving even closer to him, putting her arms around his neck, and pressing her mouth to his.

Chapter 8

Longarm might have been surprised by Kate's action, but he'd always considered himself an adaptable sort, able to go with the flow of whatever was happening around him. So when she kissed him, he just naturally put his arms around her and kissed her back.

He could feel the strength in her body as she pressed against him, but he felt her softness as well. Her lips were cool at first but built up some heat in a hurry. Her mouth tasted good.

When the kiss was over, though, it was *over*. Kate jerked her head away from Longarm's, and her eyes were wide with horror as she looked at him. She took her arms from around his neck and planted her hands against his chest. "Let go of me!" she said as she shoved away from him.

Longarm didn't try to hold her. He opened his arms so that she was free to go. She moved back so quickly that she stumbled against the chart table.

"How . . . how dare you—"

"Seemed to me it was your idea, Cap'n," Longarm said coolly. He was a little disappointed in Kate. He had never cared for women who threw themselves at a man, then acted all offended when their hair got a mite mussed.

Evidently she shared that sentiment, because she suddenly

let out a laugh of self-derision. "My God, I can't believe I just did that."

"You mean kissing me?"

She shook her head. "No, I'm talking about the way I carried on when I realized what I was doing. I acted just like the sort of prissy little milksop they tried to turn me into at that damned finishing school. I'm sorry, Custis."

Longarm relaxed and grinned. "No harm done. I reckon I can stand to have my boss grab me and kiss me ever' so often." As long as Billy Vail never tries it, he added to himself.

"Yes, but after everything I said about Ben—"

Longarm held up a hand to stop her. "No need to go into that. I've tried to help out, and you're grateful for it. That's all it amounts to."

She nodded, eager to accept his explanation. "That's right. I—"

A sudden commotion from the wharf made her stop short and turn in that direction. So did Longarm. He heard angry voices, and a moment later, as he and Kate stepped over to the big window, the blast of a gunshot sounded.

"It's McConnell!" Kate gasped as she and Longarm looked down at the mob of angry men crowding onto the wharf next to the riverboat.

Longarm turned hurriedly toward the door. There had been only one shot so far, and he didn't know who had fired it, but he wanted to get down there before things got more out of hand.

He took the ladder a couple of rungs at a time, then dropped the last few feet to the main deck. Kate wasn't far behind him. Longarm strode rapidly along the deck toward the gangplank, shouldering aside several men who stood in his way. A brief glance at them told him they were gold seekers who had already come on board the riverboat.

Muleshoe Flynn stood at the head of the gangplank, an old Dragoon Colt clutched in his hand. Gray smoke curled from the long barrel of the weapon. At the foot of the gangplank, bristling with anger, stood Ben McConnell. Ike Carpen

was beside him, and behind them were the other members of the *Yukon Queen*'s old crew.

"Put down that hogleg, you drunken old coot!" McConnell yelled at Muleshoe. "You'd damned well better let us aboard, or—"

"Or what, McConnell?" Longarm cut in as he stepped up beside Muleshoe. "You don't have any business on this boat anymore."

"You!" McConnell exclaimed. "I'd heard you signed on with Katie, you bastard. You won't ever take my place—"

"He already has," Kate said, coming up on Longarm's right. "And he's a better first mate than you ever were, Ben McConnell!"

That's it, thought Longarm. Throw a little more kerosene on the fire.

He took a deep breath and said, "You'd best move along, McConnell. You and your friends are interfering with our passengers." Several men were standing farther back along the wharf, Longarm had noted, who weren't part of the former crew. Judging from the gear they had with them, they were prospectors who wanted to book passage on the sternwheeler.

"You wouldn't have any passengers if it wasn't for me and the rest of these boys," McConnell said bitterly.

Longarm stared at him, surprised by that brazen claim. "How in blue blazes do you figure that, old son?"

Defiantly, McConnell said, "It was us who kept the boat going after Cap'n Asa passed on. *She'd* have wrecked it or lost it somehow."

Kate gasped. "That's a lie! I'm a good captain."

"You're a woman." McConnell said that as if it explained everything.

Muleshoe lifted the Dragoon. "Lemme shoot the son of a bitch," he pleaded.

"Stop waving that cannon around," Longarm snapped. As far as he could see, none of McConnell's mob were armed with guns, though a few had knives stuck in their belts. He didn't think they were foolish enough to come charging up

91

the gangplank in the face of his Colt, and he could get the revolver out in a hurry if need be. Until then, the less brandishing of firearms there was, the greater the likelihood that cooler heads would prevail.

Longarm turned his attention back to McConnell and went on, "Unless you're here to book passage to Circle City, we don't have any business with you, old son."

With a visible effort, McConnell controlled his anger. "I thought I'd try one more time to talk some sense into Katie's head. I can see now that's not going to happen. Maybe it's time we just take back what's rightfully ours." He put a foot on the bottom of the gangplank.

Longarm's hand moved toward the Colt holstered in the cross-draw rig, but before he could grasp it, a new voice called out, "I wouldn't do that if I was you, mister."

The voice belonged to Joe, the oldest of the three Yakima Indian brothers. All three of them had come around the corner of the riverboat's cabins, and they were armed for bear. Joe carried a shotgun, while each of his brothers had a long-barreled, single-shot rifle.

From the stern, Raymond Grantham shouted, "Better do as he says!"

Longarm glanced in that direction and saw Grantham and Swain standing there, each of them holding a pistol. Longarm didn't know where the guns had come from or if the youngsters had any idea of how to use them, but the odds had suddenly and dramatically increased against the mob. McConnell and the other members of the old crew still outnumbered the new one, but the guns evened things up considerable, Longarm judged.

McConnell stayed where he was, with one foot on the gangplank, for a long moment. His hands clenched into fists and a muscle in his jaw jumped around a little. But he managed to keep a tight rein on his temper, and after a moment he glanced back at Ike Carpen. The burly Carpen shrugged and said, "They're holdin' better cards, Ben. Nothin' we can do." He glanced at Longarm and added in a menacing tone, "This time."

"All right," McConnell said. He looked straight at Kate Ridgway and went on, "If that's the way you want to play this, Katie, then so be it. We'll beat you at your own game."

"What are you talking about, McConnell?" Kate demanded.

Longarm had a pretty good idea what McConnell was going to say next. The man confirmed it by declaring, "We'll just get a boat of our own and show you that you don't have any business taking that old coffee mill up the Yukon." He turned his head and raised his voice. "All you gents who're bound for Circle City better listen to me! You'll get there sooner if you wait and book passage with Captain Ben McConnell!"

"You're crazy!" Kate said. "You don't even have a boat!"

"Not right now," McConnell shot back at her, "but the *Lone Pine* is due in tomorrow."

From the corner of his mouth, Longarm asked Kate, "What's the *Lone Pine*?"

"One of the other riverboats," she replied grimly. "And the man who owns it has been looking for somebody to buy it."

Longarm grimaced. It looked like fate was conspiring to let Ben McConnell continue making an annoyance of himself.

"You don't have enough money to buy the *Lone Pine*," Kate said scathingly to McConnell.

"We'll just see about that," he replied confidently. "Between the whole bunch of us, I'll just bet we do." He backed away from the gangplank. "Come on, boys, we've got work to do. All you other fellas, you remember what I said. We'll get you to the gold first!"

"We'll have a day's head start!" Kate called after him.

McConnell shook his head. "Not good enough. We'll make that up and pass you."

"All right, then!" Kate blazed. "If it's a race you want, then it's a damned race you'll get!"

Longarm bit back a groan. This wasn't working out the way he wanted it at all. All he'd had in mind was getting to

Circle City as fast as he could so that he could find Harrison Dodge and arrest the little son of a bitch. Now he found himself getting mixed up in some sort of riverboat race that was bound to increase the bad blood between Kate and McConnell.

He hoped she wouldn't be so anxious to beat her former first mate that she pushed the *Yukon Queen* so hard its boilers blew up.

McConnell and his cronies moved off down the wharf and onto the shore, and Longarm noticed that several of the gold seekers who had been waiting to board the *Yukon Queen* followed him. Those men were taking a chance that McConnell would even be able to lay his hands on a boat, let alone beat Kate's vessel to Circle City, but sometimes when men were caught up in the grip of gold fever, they didn't think everything through.

At any rate, Longarm wasn't going to go chasing after them, begging them to book passage on the sternwheeler. Instead, he motioned for the Indians and the two youngsters from back East to join him and Kate near the gangplank.

"Where'd you get the arsenal?" Longarm asked as Grantham and Swain walked up carrying the pistols.

"They gave them to us," Grantham said, nodding toward the trio of Indians.

Joe smiled. "And it's a good thing you didn't have to use them. They haven't been fired in years. They might have blown up in your hands."

Swain gulped. "Now you tell us."

Longarm regarded Joe intently. "So you were bluffing?"

Joe shrugged and said, "White men aren't the only ones who know how to play games."

His brother Pete added, "Anyway, it wasn't just a bluff. These rifles and Joe's greener work just fine."

"And so does this old Dragoon o' mine," Muleshoe put in. "Been carryin' it ever since I rode with ol' Cap'n John Hays and fit the Comanch' at Bandera Pass."

Longarm considered it unlikely that Muleshoe had been with Captain John Coffee Hays and the Texas Rangers at the

Battle of Bandera Pass, but he didn't argue the point. He said, "Everybody put the artillery away and get back to work." A glance at the shore told him that McConnell and the others had disappeared into one of the saloons. "There's still plenty to do before we shove off."

McConnell's attempt to lure passengers away from the *Yukon Queen* was only partially successful. By the middle of the afternoon, forty-one men had paid for their passage and come aboard the riverboat with their gear, bound for Circle City. That seemed to be all the passengers, however, so the boat would be leaving St. Michael without being completely booked.

Still, Longarm figured, the fares would be enough to pay the crew and cover the other expenses of the voyage, with enough left over to make a healthy profit for Kate. He was anxious to leave the port settlement behind him and so was she, so after a brief consultation in the wheelhouse, they decided the time had come.

The boilers were hot and steam was up. Longarm checked to make sure everyone was on board who intended to make the trip, then waved to Pete and Carl, who waited on the wharf. They untied the thick ropes binding the boat to the dock and jumped aboard, then took up heavy poles and pushed the vessel clear. Joe was in the engine room, and when Kate called down to him through the speaking tube, he pushed the throttle forward and engaged the paddlewheel. The giant wheel at the stern of the boat began to turn, slowly at first and then faster and faster, churning the waters of Norton Sound as it backed away from the wharf.

Longarm went up to the wheelhouse. Kate was at the helm, her hands resting easily on the large, brightly polished wooden wheel. She glanced back over her shoulder, saw Longarm standing there, and gave him a determined nod. "Take the speaking tube," she ordered.

"Yes, ma'am, Cap'n," he replied.

Kate spun the wheel and said, "All stop."

"All stop," Longarm repeated into the speaking tube.

The paddlewheel ground to a halt.

"Ahead one-half," Kate ordered. Longarm repeated the command into the rubber tube, and the wheel began to turn in the other direction, biting into the water and sending the boat forward. The speed increased steadily until the *Yukon Queen* was steaming easily along the shoreline of the peninsula on which St. Michael was located.

The estuary was so wide it was like part of the sound at first, but gradually the shores drew in so that the stream began to look more like a river. Longarm went to the door of the wheelhouse and looked astern. The settlement was barely visible in the distance. Another few minutes and he wouldn't be able to see it anymore.

That was all right with him. St. Michael had been only a stop along the way, and while he had enjoyed the time he spent there with the blond prostitute Caroline, he was more than ready to leave.

Somewhere up ahead in the vast Alaskan wilderness was the reason he had come here in the first place, the fugitive named Harrison Dodge. Longarm turned away from St. Michael and once more looked where he was going, rather than where he had been.

Summer in Alaska meant that the days were long, with only a few hours of darkness each night. So the *Yukon Queen* was able to steam along for quite a while after leaving St. Michael before the gathering shadows forced it to stop and tie up at the riverbank.

The river was just that now. The sternwheeler was miles inland, well on its way to the point where the smaller stream joined the main branch of the Yukon. The stream was some twenty yards wide at this point, flanked by the low plains that were dotted here and there with clumps of brush and scrubby trees. For the most part, however, the landscape was rather barren.

Kate chose a spot where some spruce trees grew close to the river. Joe, Pete, and Carl jumped ashore with the ropes and tied up. Longarm had been impressed so far with the

three brothers. As fishermen, they knew their way around boats. Being able to hire them had been a stroke of luck.

Their father Yak was still in a semi-stupor and hadn't been good for much of anything so far, but Longarm still had hopes that he would be later on, once more of the liquor was out of his system. He'd had Muleshoe go through Yak's gear, just to make sure the Indian hadn't smuggled any hooch on board.

The two college boys, Grantham and Swain, still weren't completely recovered from their hangovers, but they mustered up enough enthusiasm and willingness to work so that Longarm didn't regret hiring them. They were utterly ignorant of what hard labor was really about, of course, but they would learn. By the time they reached Circle City they would have calluses on their hands and muscles that hadn't been there before. If anything, the experience of working on the riverboat would actually improve their chances of being able to find gold and make that fortune they were after.

Muleshoe had labored mightily in the boat's galley all afternoon, and by evening he had a supper of sourdough biscuits, molasses, and caribou steaks whipped up. He had beans soaking, he reported, so the next day they would be ready to cook. The fare was simple but fairly tasty, and Longarm thought the old man had done a pretty good job, considering that he was having to cook for over fifty people.

After everyone had eaten and most of the lamps on board had been extinguished, Longarm took a last turn around the deck to make sure everything was all right. A glance upward told him that a lantern was still burning in the wheelhouse, so he climbed the ladder and stepped into the shacklike structure.

Kate was bent over the chart table, studying a map that was spread out before her. She glanced up at Longarm and asked, "Everything shipshape?"

"Seems to be," he said. He came over to the table and perched one hip on the corner of it. He pointed at the chart and asked, "Figuring out our route?"

"Just refreshing my mind. There's not that much figuring

to do," she said. She traced a line on the map with her fingertip. "This is the stream we're on now. In a couple of days, we'll hit the main branch of the Yukon. We follow it north, then northeast, then finally it takes a turn to the southeast and runs on to Circle City, almost at the Canadian border, here. The river follows the valleys through the mountains, so that's not a problem."

"What about rapids?"

Kate shook her head. "A few bad places, but there are channels around them. This boat doesn't require much draft. That's why it's good for rivers like the Yukon."

Longarm had been on other riverboats that had gone up the Missouri and Yellowstone Rivers, so he knew what she was talking about. This trip seemed like it was going to be very similar to those voyages.

"How far are we talking about?"

"It's a little more than seven hundred miles," Kate said. "It'll take us between two and three weeks."

Longarm did some quick figuring. "And two or three weeks back to St. Michael . . . shoot, that's almost the end of summer!"

She nodded. "Yes, this will probably be the last trip this season. Three to four trips per summer is the best we can do. You don't want to be halfway between Circle City and St. Michael when ice starts to form on the Yukon. If you get caught like that, you might as well get ready to spend a long, cold winter in the middle of nowhere."

Kate rolled up the chart and put it away in a drawer. She didn't seem to be in any hurry to leave, so Longarm took out a cheroot and put it unlit in his mouth. "Is this the first year you've been making the runs to Circle City without your pa?"

"Yes, he passed away during the winter. We have a home down in Sitka and spend the winters there. Spent the winters there, I should say, since he's gone now."

Her voice was matter-of-fact, as if she had done her grieving and moved on, but Longarm suspected that some pain

still lurked inside her. Kate just wasn't the type to let it out very easily.

"How many years before that did he come up here?"

"Twelve," Kate replied. "Ever since I was fourteen." She smiled. "Before that he took the old girl up and down the Columbia River. She was the *Columbia Queen* then."

It took Longarm a second to realize she was talking about the riverboat. He asked, "Why the move to Alaska?"

"It was a new frontier. You wouldn't think it to look at him, but my father had a lot of pioneer in him. He wasn't the sort to settle down in one place for a long time. Of course, he felt like he had to, because he was raising a daughter by himself, but every so often he just had to move on."

Longarm nodded. "Sounds like he was a good man."

"He was," Kate said softly. "He was a very good man. But he left awfully big shoes to fill."

"Nothing says you have to fill 'em," Longarm pointed out. "I didn't know your pa, but he sounds like the sort of fella who'd want his daughter to be happy, no matter whether she was carrying on for him or not."

"That's just it. The boat *does* make me happy. I've never been happier anywhere else than right here. I can't imagine doing anything else."

Longarm nodded. "Then you should keep at it."

"I intend to." Kate squared her shoulders. "And Ben McConnell can just go to hell."

Longarm grinned. His main goal was still to find and arrest Harrison Dodge . . . but if he could lend a hand to Kate Ridgway in the process and help her hold on to her dream, then so much the better.

Early the next morning, as the *Yukon Queen* was getting underway, another boat came around a bend in the river and steamed toward them, the paddlewheel on its stern throwing water high in the air as it revolved.

Longarm climbed to the wheelhouse as the two boats met and passed each other. Kate blew the *Yukon Queen*'s whistle, and the other vessel responded in kind.

"That'd be the *Lone Pine*, I reckon," Longarm said as he came up beside Kate.

She nodded. "That's right. She'll be in St. Michael before the day's over. But even if McConnell strikes a deal with the owner as soon as the boat docks, it'll be tomorrow before he can get started after us. We'll have more than a day's lead on him."

"Can he make that up?"

"Not unless we run into some trouble along the way," Kate replied, but Longarm thought she didn't sound quite as confident as she could have.

The *Yukon Queen* was a pretty old boat, he thought. From what he had seen of the *Lone Pine*, it was newer and somewhat larger, which meant its engine might be more powerful, as well. He was no expert on boats, but he had the feeling that if McConnell really wanted to push it, he might be able to catch and pass Kate's boat before they reached Circle City.

As far as his assignment was concerned, it didn't really matter which vessel got to Circle City first, he reminded himself. Catching up to Harrison Dodge was the only important thing.

But Longarm was only human, and whether he liked it or not, his competitive urges had been aroused by his run-ins with Ben McConnell. He didn't want the redhead to get the best of Kate Ridgway.

Besides, winning the race would mean that he had gotten to Circle City the fastest way possible.

By the time they reached the main branch of the Yukon and turned north along it, the coastal plains had given way to low hills studded with spruce and cedar. Mountains were visible to the east and north, like long lines of humpbacked blue elephants in the distance. Occasionally, Longarm could make out the white caps of snow that topped most of the peaks.

Grantham, Swain, Joe, Pete, and Carl took turns stoking the boilers. Longarm and Yak spelled them as needed. After a few sessions around the boilers, Yak seemed to be more clearheaded, though he was still sullen most of the time. As

Grover Hanratty had predicted, Yak had had to sweat the remaining liquor out of his system.

Muleshoe continued cooking and surprised Longarm with his skill in that area. And although the crotchety old-timer wouldn't have admitted it for the world, Longarm thought he was pretty happy to be doing something worthwhile again, rather than cadging drinks in a saloon and trying to sell gold mine maps to gullible treasure seekers.

As for Longarm himself, he took a few turns at the wheel while the *Yukon Queen* was chugging along broad, peaceful stretches of the river. Other than that, his job consisted of making sure that everything else was going all right. There were times he felt downright useless.

As the days passed, the landscape along the river grew more rugged. The hills rose more steeply from the banks, and the trees were thicker and taller. It was beginning to be pretty country, reminding Longarm of places he had been in the Rockies and the Sierras.

There were a few settlements between St. Michael and Circle City, Kate informed him, all of them small and crude. But the boat would tie up at all of them, and as it did, Longarm would have to check and make sure Harrison Dodge hadn't stopped off at any of these smaller settlements. He considered that unlikely, but he wouldn't have thought that a city fella like Dodge would run off up here to this Alaskan wilderness, either. A gent was liable to do almost anything when he was running for his life, whether it was something expected of him or not.

The first settlement was nothing but a trading post and a few Indian lodges, and the trader told Longarm he hadn't seen anybody matching Dodge's description all summer. Longarm wasn't surprised by that. The *Yukon Queen* moved on upriver and a few days later came to another settlement where the Yukon swung back to the east. This place was called Burke's Bar, Kate informed Longarm, after a sandbar in the river and the man who had built a trading post on shore opposite it. After the riverboat was tied up securely,

Kate and Longarm went ashore, and she introduced him to the trader.

Burke was a tall, thin man with a rust-colored beard. "Pleased to meet you," he said as he shook hands with Longarm. "What happened to Ben?"

"McConnell's not my first mate anymore," Kate replied grimly. "Seems he decided he didn't want to work for a woman."

Burke clucked his tongue. "Damn fool if you ask me. You goin' to stay on the river, Mr. Long, or are you one of those so-called Argonauts?"

Longarm smiled and said, "I'm bound for Circle City to meet up with my partner, but I figured it wouldn't hurt to give Kate a hand along the way." Innocently, he went on, "Maybe you saw my pard when he was on his way through here a while back. Little fella, not much hair—"

"Name of Dodge, right?" Burke interrupted.

Longarm felt his pulse quicken. "That's right. You know him?"

"Yeah, he came in here a couple of weeks ago when the *Samuel Jennings* stopped for the night."

"That's the other riverboat that makes the Yukon run," Kate told Longarm.

He'd already figured that out, but he nodded his thanks. "Ol' Dodge ain't still here, is he?" he asked Burke.

"Oh, no, he left the next morning when the boat did." Burke frowned. "Have you worked with that gent before, Mr. Long? Truth to tell, he didn't seem much like the sort to be looking for gold."

"He's tougher than he looks," Longarm said.

"Well, he ought to be in Circle City by now. Hope you find him."

"I'm sure I will."

The confirmation that he was truly on Dodge's trail made Longarm feel better. It was just a matter of time now, he told himself, before he had the fugitive in custody . . .

"Captain Ridgway! Mr. Long!"

Longarm and Kate swung around in surprise as they heard

their names called in an urgent voice. They saw Raymond Grantham come hurrying into the trading post, trailed as usual by his friend Timothy Swain. Both young men were wide-eyed, and they both started babbling as they came up to Longarm and Kate.

"Hold on, hold on," Longarm told them sharply. "Only one of you can eat the apple at a time. Now, Raymond, what the hell's goin' on?"

Grantham caught his breath as he pointed downriver. "They're coming," he said. "Another boat."

"It's that man McConnell," Swain said excitedly. "I saw him, standing on the front of the boat."

Kate's breath hissed between her teeth. "Already?" she said in a hollow voice. "He's caught up to us already?"

Longarm took hold of her arm. "Come on," he said. "Let's go see how bad it is."

Chapter 9

Bad enough, Longarm saw as he and Kate stepped onto the porch of Burke's trading post.

A sternwheeler he recognized as the *Lone Pine* was indeed steaming up the Yukon. Ben McConnell, a fur cap on his unruly red hair, stood on the bow, a rifle cradled in his arms. Several other men stood with him, similarly armed. Longarm looked up at the wheelhouse and saw Ike Carpen's squat figure standing at the wheel. Men lined the rails on both sides of the deck, most of them gold seekers from the *Bowman* who had chosen to wait for McConnell rather than trusting their luck with Kate and the *Yukon Queen*.

"That bastard," Kate said, as much to herself as to Longarm. "He really did it."

"Did you think he wouldn't?"

She shook her head. "No, I knew he was prideful enough—and fool enough—to carry out his threat. But I didn't think he could possibly catch up to us this fast. He must have been running at night. That's the only way he could have done it."

Longarm nodded. If it meant getting the best of Kate Ridgway, then he didn't doubt for a second that McConnell would run the risk of steaming up the river in the dark.

Kate broke into a run toward the rough wharf where the *Yukon Queen* was tied up. "Come on!" she shouted over her

shoulder to Longarm. "We've got to push off right away!"

He sighed, but he hurried after her. For better or worse, he was part of this race now.

And a real race it was. Kate's shouts got everybody back on board the riverboat in a hurry, and the engine still had steam up, but it took time to cast off, shove away from the bank, and back into the river. By the time Longarm relayed Kate's order of "All ahead full!" over the speaking tube to Joe in the engine room, the *Lone Pine* was less than a hundred yards behind the *Yukon Queen*.

Longarm spotted Yak on deck and leaned over to call down to him through the wheelhouse window. "Find out how full the fireboxes are!"

Yak waved his hand in understanding and went below-decks. A few minutes later, he reappeared and climbed to the wheel house.

"Boxes half full, no more," he told Longarm.

Kate heard the report and exclaimed, "Damn it! I was counting on filling them up at Burke's. Now we'll have to stop for wood somewhere up ahead."

Longarm eyed the trees growing thickly on the banks of the Yukon. "Looks like there's plenty of it," he said.

"Yes, but it'll have to be cut! That takes time. We could've filled the boxes at Burke's and taken just the time needed to load them. This will slow us down."

Longarm looked back through the open door of the wheelhouse at the *Lone Pine*. "McConnell didn't stop, either. Won't he need wood?"

"We don't know how much he has on board. He could have stocked up somewhere downriver. Damn and blast!"

The engines were running full-bore. Longarm could hear their rumble and feel their vibration in the planks underneath his feet. So far during this voyage, Kate had run the engines at three-quarter speed a lot of time, but never full out like this. Longarm had heard of steamboat boilers exploding when they were pushed too hard and run too hot; he didn't want such a fate to overtake the *Yukon Queen*, even if it meant losing the race to McConnell.

He suggested, "Maybe you'd better tell Joe to throttle back a mite—"

"Hell, no!" Kate cried. "Then McConnell would pass us for sure."

Longarm looked back at the *Lone Pine* again. It had closed the gap somewhat, so that now only fifty yards separated the two sternwheelers.

"I'm sorry, Kate," he said. "It looks like he's going to pass us no matter what we do."

"What?" She twisted her head around so that she could see the other boat. "Damnation!"

The vibration in the floor had grown worse. It felt to Longarm as if the whole blasted boat was shaking now. He couldn't catch Harrison Dodge if he was blown sky-high. He didn't want to do it, but if he had to he would reveal his identity as a federal lawman and *order* Kate to slow down.

Suddenly, she bent her head as she tightly gripped the wheel. Longarm saw a shudder go through her. He stepped forward and saw the shine of tears on her cheeks. In a choked voice, she said, "Ahead one-half."

Longarm grabbed the speaking tube and called, "Joe! Throttle back to one-half!"

Joe didn't respond, but a couple of seconds later, Longarm heard the roar of the engines grow a bit softer, and the shaking under his feet subsided somewhat. The landscape along the riverbanks quit rushing by so fast. Gradually, the engines smoothed out into their usual regular pulsations.

Longarm heard faint cheering.

He looked to the right and saw the *Lone Pine* pulling even with the *Yukon Queen*. The passengers and crew of McConnell's boat were shouting enthusiastically as it caught up with the other vessel. Longarm felt a twinge of sympathy as he looked at Kate, who was still hunched over the wheel with her eyes fixed straight ahead on the river, rather than looking at the other boat.

"I couldn't let her blow up," Kate said, despair and defeat in her voice. "I just couldn't."

"You did the only thing you could," Longarm told her.

"But I'm sorry, Kate. You didn't deserve to lose—"

"That son of a bitch!" Kate broke in. She leaned forward. *"Look!"*

The *Lone Pine* was pulling ahead now, its paddle throwing water high in the air as it revolved too fast for the eye to follow. On the boat's port side, just ahead of the stern, the old name had been painted over, and a new name now adorned the vessel.

McConnell had renamed his boat the *Katie.*

"That no-good . . . lousy . . . he knows I hate that name!" the real Kate wailed. She jerked her head around to glare at Longarm. "All ahead—"

"No." He knew what she was about to say. She was about to order full speed again. "I won't do it," Longarm went on. "If you want to blow up this boat, you can tell Joe yourself." He stepped away from the speaking tube.

Kate glared at him and said, "Damn it, Custis, is this another mutiny?"

"Call it what you want. I know you're the cap'n and I'm only the first mate, but I won't help you blow this boat and everybody on it to Kingdom Come."

For a second he thought she was going to grab the speaking tube and give the order herself, but then her shoulders slumped and she said, "You're right. All we can do is let them go."

She looked so despondent Longarm felt like stepping over to her and putting his arm around her shoulders to comfort her. He knew that if he did that, she was liable to kick him in the shin or punch him in the belly, but he almost followed through on the impulse anyway.

What stopped him was the bullet that whined past his head and thudded into something behind him.

Longarm hadn't heard a shot, but he knew all too well the sound of a slug ripping through the air near his ear. He lunged forward and grabbed Kate, then fell with her to the floor of the wheelhouse. She cried out in shock and pain as they struck the floor. Longarm said, "Stay down!" The walls of the wheelhouse weren't overly thick and might not stop a

rifle bullet, but they were better cover than nothing.

He heard a groan and turned his head to see Yak sitting with his back against the wall beside the door. He had almost forgotten that the Indian was there, but now he was reminded of it quite vividly, because the bullet that had missed Longarm had struck Yak. A bloodstain spread down the front of the flannel shirt from Yak's left shoulder.

Longarm scrambled over to him. "How bad are you hit?"

Yak shook his head. He was conscious and seemed to be fully aware of what was going on. "Don't know," he grunted. "Hurts like hell."

Longarm ripped the Indian's shirt open and saw that the bullet had entered just below the left shoulder and ripped through the fleshy part of Yak's upper side, under the left arm. It was a messy, no doubt painful wound, but if no bones were broken it might not be too serious. Longarm tore the shirt again, this time making a pad out of the flannel.

"Hold this on there," he said as he slapped the makeshift compress over the entrance wound. Yak did so while Longarm examined the exit wound. It was a little bigger and bleeding just as bad.

"Don't feel too good," Yak said. His eyes threatened to roll up in his head. Longarm knew he was on the verge of passing out.

"Let me help," Kate said as she crawled over to them.

"Ever patch up a bullet wound?" Longarm asked her.

"As a matter of fact, I have," she said, and Longarm thought that he shouldn't have been surprised at that answer. By this time, nothing Kate Ridgway said or did could surprise him all that much.

He eased Yak forward so that Kate could get another compress on the exit wound, then they used the Indian's belt to tie the crude bandages in place. Yak was only half-conscious by now. Longarm leaned him back against the wall gently. Yak muttered incomprehensibly.

"Someone took a *shot* at us," Kate said, sounding as if she could hardly believe it.

"Yep, they sure did," Longarm agreed. "I heard it go past

me and then hit Yak. That means it came from somewhere up ahead of us."

"McConnell," Kate breathed. "I didn't think he would . . . that lowdown . . ."

"It might not have been McConnell," Longarm said, "but I reckon from where I was standing and where Yak was standing, the shot had to come from the *Lone Pine*. I mean, the—"

"Leave it at that," Kate said. "And McConnell had a rifle. I saw him with it!"

"He was on the bow when the boat passed us," Longarm pointed out. "Of course, I reckon he could've come back to the stern. But it could have been somebody else." For what it was worth, taking a potshot at the *Yukon Queen* sounded to him like something Ike Carpen would do, but Longarm didn't say that. He had no proof Carpen was to blame for wounding Yak.

No one had been at the wheel for several moments now. Longarm said, "Stay here," to Kate, then came up in a crouch and went to the front of the wheelhouse. He raised up enough to peer out the open front window. With the riverboat's engines cut back, it had fallen steadily farther behind McConnell's boat. The newly christened *Katie* was more than a hundred yards ahead now. Longarm saw men clustered around the stern, but at this distance, he couldn't tell who they were or if they were armed.

"I reckon there was just the one shot," he said. "Doesn't look like they're up to anything else."

"You'd better go get Yak's sons, so they can take care of him," Kate said. She stood up and moved forward. "I'll take the wheel."

Longarm hesitated, then nodded. He left the wheelhouse and went down the ladder to the main deck, which was crowded with passengers. They had been caught up in the competition between the two riverboats, too. None of them paid any attention to Longarm, and he realized that down here, the men probably were unaware that a shot had been fired at the wheelhouse. They wouldn't have been able to

109

hear it at that distance, over the noise of the engines.

Yak's boys were down in the engine room. Longarm went to get them, wondering as he descended belowdecks just who had pulled the trigger on the shot that had wounded the Indian.

"Damn it!" Ben McConnell shouted as he ripped the rifle out of Ike Carpen's hands. "What did you think you were doing, Ike? You could've hit Katie!"

"I aimed high," Carpen said defensively. "I just wanted to throw a scare into 'em, Ben, so they'd go ahead and give up. I never wanted to hurt the girl."

"Well, you could have," McConnell raged. He looked like he wanted to throw Carpen's rifle overboard, but he restrained himself and handed the weapon to one of the other men instead.

Several members of the crew were standing on the after deck of the riverboat. McConnell had come back here to watch the *Yukon Queen* as they left it behind, maybe rub Kate Ridgway's nose in her defeat by waving to her, but he had let out a startled shout when he saw Carpen lowering a rifle. Powdersmoke had been curling from the barrel of the weapon. For a second, McConnell had seen red. He wanted to beat Kate at her own game, wanted her to see the foolishness of insisting that she could be a riverboat captain, but he didn't want her to get hurt.

"It doesn't matter whether they give up or not," McConnell said as he calmed down a little. "They're not going to be able to catch us."

"You don't know that," Carpen said. "Something could happen to slow us down."

McConnell shook his head. "No, this race is over. Our boat is faster. Now that we've caught the *Yukon Queen*, we won't have any trouble staying ahead of her."

"You talkin' about the boat—or the girl?"

McConnell glared at Carpen. The short, burly Carpen was a good riverboat man, a damned good one, but sometimes McConnell wasn't sure he really knew the man. He ignored

110

Carpen's insolent question and ordered, "No more shooting." He looked around at the other crew members and raised his voice so that all of them could hear him over the rumble of the engines. "Does everybody understand? No more shooting!"

There were nods of agreement all around.

Satisfied, McConnell turned back toward the wheelhouse. The Yukon wasn't the trickiest river in the world to navigate, but it had its challenges like all streams, and he wanted to be at the wheel to handle them.

Carpen waited until McConnell had gone up the ladder and into the wheelhouse before he jerked his rifle away from the man holding it. "You heard Ben, Ike," the man said. "No more potshots at the *Yukon Queen*."

"I heard him, all right," Carpen growled. He rubbed his hard, stubbly jaw, knowing full well that he had put that shot into the wheelhouse on purpose, hoping that he'd hit somebody. "But one of these days, *Cap'n* Ben McConnell's gonna find out that he's given one order too many."

Longarm helped Joe, Pete, and Carl carry their father down to the cabin Longarm had been using. As captain and first mate, Kate and Longarm had cabins to themselves, but the rest of the crew slept on deck or in the engine room or galley. The three young men were upset that Yak had been shot, but once they had placed him in the bunk and finished taking his shirt off, they saw that the wound wasn't too bad. Carl got some rags and water and removed the temporary bandages. He started cleaning the wounds while Pete looked on.

Joe went out on deck with Longarm. The young man's face was grim as he asked, "Who did this?"

Longarm shook his head. "I don't know. I'm pretty sure the shot came from McConnell's boat, but there's no telling who fired it."

"It must have been McConnell."

"I wouldn't be too sure about that," Longarm cautioned. "There are a lot of people on that boat. It could've been any of them, even one of the passengers."

"Why would any of them want to shoot my father?"

"Well, now . . . I don't reckon that bullet was aimed at Yak, old son. He just happened to be standing in the wrong place at the wrong time. I heard the slug go past my head before it hit him."

Joe's eyes widened. "Then someone on board that boat was trying to kill you."

"Not necessarily. Kate was up there in the wheelhouse, too. I think whoever fired the shot was just trying to discourage us."

Joe shook his head. "The race is lost. We cannot keep up with that other boat."

"Nope, I reckon not. But we can go on to Circle City anyway. This'll be the *Yukon Queen*'s last trip this season. Next summer, though, if you want to sign on again, I reckon Cap'n Ridgway would be glad to have you. I know for a fact she's been pleased with the work you and your brothers have done."

"We will think on it," Joe said with a solemn nod. "What of McConnell?"

Longarm's gaze narrowed as he looked upriver. The *Katie* was still visible, though the gap between the two boats had widened to several hundred yards by now.

"If he's still in Circle City when we get there," Longarm said. "I intend to have me a little talk with Mr. Ben McConnell."

By evening, the *Katie* was no longer in sight, having gone on around several bends in the river far ahead of the *Yukon Queen*. Though Longarm hated for Kate to lose the race to McConnell, he was just as glad to see the last of the other boat. This way, the next week or so might pass peacefully as they made their way on to their destination.

Kate put in to the riverbank while there was still some light in the sky. "We'll go ashore and start chopping wood for the fireboxes," she told Longarm as the boat was being tied up. "There's no point in hurrying anymore."

"I'll break out the axes," he agreed.

A short time later, the forest along the river rang with the sound of steel biting into tree trunks. Carl stayed on board the boat to look after Yak, but Joe and Pete went ashore, along with Longarm, Raymond Grantham, and Timothy Swain. Neither of the two college men had ever chopped down trees before. Longarm found himself hoping that neither of them missed a swing and chopped off a foot. After that nearly happened a couple of times, he took the axes away from them and put them to work carrying logs out of the forest and piling them on the riverbank. Once the stack was large enough, Joe and Pete got a crosscut saw from the boat and began sawing the logs into more manageable lengths. Longarm found himself a good stump from a previous cutting, propped the short lengths of wood on it, and started splitting them. Grantham and Swain picked up the pieces and carried them on board the boat to fill the fireboxes.

It was hard work, all the way around, and Longarm found himself sweating. He took off his coat, then his flannel shirt, and swung the axe wearing just his long underwear above the waist.

Kate came along and watched him for a few minutes, then said, "You look like you've done some log-splitting before."

Longarm grinned. "Yeah, me and ol' Abe Lincoln, we've split our share of logs."

Kate frowned at him and asked, "You didn't really know Lincoln, did you?"

"Nope," Longarm said with a chuckle. "I fought in his war, though. Just don't bother asking me which side I was on. I disremember."

"I was just a child. I don't recall much about the war. It didn't really affect us much in Oregon and Washington."

Longarm swung the axe, felt the satisfying shiver of impact up his arms to his shoulders as another piece of log split. He enjoyed talking with Kate, but he didn't have much breath for it at the moment.

"Do you think anyone will book passage on the *Yukon Queen* next summer once word gets around that McConnell beat us?" she asked.

Longarm paused and leaned on the axe. "Next summer's a long way off," he said. "Chances are, most folks will have forgotten all about it by then. You've got the makings of a good crew here. Add a few more next summer and you'll be fine."

Kate smiled at him. "Thank you, Custis. I don't know if you're right or not, but I appreciate the sentiment."

After night fell, the men worked by lanternlight until the fireboxes were full, then ate a cold supper and rolled in blankets on the deck to catch a few hours of sleep before it was time to push off again. Longarm took a final walk around the boat before turning in himself. He liked to be sure that everything was secure for the night.

He was on the bow of the boat when he heard a faint ripple in the water that struck him as odd. Thinking it might be a large fish of some sort, he paused and leaned on the railing to look out over the dark expanse of the Yukon. On the other side of the river, a thickly wooded ridge rose steeply, looming up over the water so that it cast stygian shadows over half the stream.

Longarm didn't see anything, didn't hear any other strange sounds. He shrugged and turned away from the rail. His muscles ached from the hours of swinging an axe. It was going to feel good to stretch out in his bunk. He went around the front corner of the cabins, bound for the one he used. He stopped to feel inside the pocket of his shirt for a cheroot.

On the other side of the boat, the starboard side, a tiny splash sounded.

Longarm frowned and forgot about the cheroot. There was *something* in the water. He was convinced of that now. He swung around and moved quietly toward the starboard side of the *Yukon Queen*. He stopped at the corner of the cabins, took off his Stetson, and edged his head forward for a look-see. The deck was ten feet wide between the cabins and the railing, and he could see all the way to the stern of the boat. Nothing moved anywhere. The deck was empty, because all the passengers and crew sleeping in the open were on the port side, closer to shore where there was less wind.

But about halfway along the deck, there were dark spots on the planks. Longarm stared at the marks for a second before he realized what they were.

Wet footprints.

Someone had just come out of the river onto the *Yukon Queen*.

Longarm's hand went to his gun, and he palmed out the Colt as he started along the deck toward the footprints. Whoever was skulking around was going to regret it. He reached the prints and began following them toward the stern.

He had gone only a few feet before something suddenly crashed into the back of his head, knocking him forward onto his knees. Shadows darker than the deepest night rose around him and folded him into their grasp.

Chapter 10

Longarm lost consciousness for only a second. The pain of the rough planks pressing against his face roused him. Alarm bells were going off in his head—along with the usual fireworks from being walloped—and he pushed himself up and threw himself to the side in a roll. Something hit the deck with a solid *chock!* right where his head had been a second earlier. He saw someone looming over him and raised his leg, lashing out with a kick.

The heel of his boot caught his attacker on the knee. The man yelled in pain and surprise as his leg went out from under him. Longarm took advantage of the respite to roll over again and come up on one knee.

His hands were empty. He had dropped his Colt when he was clobbered from behind. The .41 derringer he usually carried in his vest was safely stowed away in his gear since he was wearing range garb now, not a suit, so the little gun couldn't save his bacon as it had so many times in the past. His rifle was in his cabin, too. He was so angry about being attacked that he was willing to take on his assailant bare-handed, but with his head so woozy from the blow it had received, that might not be a good idea.

He wasn't going to have to fight with anybody. The man he had kicked scrambled up, ran to the rail, and vaulted over it, landing in the river with a huge splash. He began swim-

ming away from the boat, heading for the opposite bank. Whatever the gent's motives might have been for sneaking aboard the *Yukon Queen*, getting into a brawl with Longarm wasn't one of them.

Longarm gave a shake of his head, clearing away the rest of the cobwebs clogging his brain. He spotted starlight glinting on his pistol where it lay a few feet away on the deck. He scooped it up and came to his feet, swaying a little as another wave of dizziness hit him and then receded.

He looked at the wet footprints on the deck and realized there were *two* sets of them. One of them led into the shadows where the man who had jumped him waited for him, while the other went on down the deck toward the stern.

That meant one of the intruders was still on board.

Longarm started toward the spot where he had been struck down, then stopped short as he realized that an axe was stuck in the deck, its handle sticking up in the air. That sound he'd heard as he rolled aside was the blade biting into the deck and getting stuck in the planking. If he hadn't moved . . . if that blow had landed as the man who struck it intended . . .

Coldness touched Longarm's spine. He had come damned close to having an axe buried in his brain.

The chill of that realization rapidly heated up into anger. The man who had tried to bust open his head with an axe might be gone, but whoever had come aboard with him was still here. Longarm slid silently along the deck, all his senses alert for any sign of the intruder.

He was almost to the paddlewheel when he saw a moving shadow near it. The man had his arms upraised and was holding something in his hand. That something was an axe, Longarm realized, and it was poised to come smashing down on one of the shafts that drove the great wheel.

Longarm lifted the Colt and eared back the hammer. The .45 was a double-action, so he really didn't need to cock it before firing, but he'd found that the sounds of a hammer being drawn back and a cylinder revolving made most men sit up and pay attention.

"I wouldn't do that, old son," he said.

The intruder caught his breath and froze for a second. Longarm thought the man was going to surrender, but suddenly the figure twisted and the arms lashed out, flinging the axe. It whipped through the air at Longarm, who said, "Shit!" and ducked for all he was worth. The axe spun past him, over his head, and clattered onto the deck.

A heartbeat later, the intruder crashed into Longarm, bowling him over. The gun in Longarm's hand blasted as his finger clenched involuntarily on the trigger, but he didn't know if he'd hit anything. He had his arms full of twisting, writhing, flailing intruder. The man tagged him with a lucky punch on the chin that bounced the back of Longarm's head off the deck. The earlier blow in the same place had left Longarm's noggin smarting, and this new impact set skyrockets off behind his eyes for the second time tonight. If this kept up, his skull was going to get downright mushy, he thought grimly.

The intruder was on top of him. Longarm's left arm shot up, and his hand found the man's throat. Longarm's fingers closed hard around it. The intruder hammered a punch into Longarm's midsection, but the big lawman hung on. He heaved up with his shoulders and rolled the man off him, slamming the man down onto the deck. Now Longarm had the advantage. He swung the gun in his other hand and felt the barrel thud into his opponent's skull. The man went limp, lying half underneath Longarm.

The errant gunshot had roused some of the people on the boat, especially those sleeping on the deck. Footsteps pounded toward Longarm as he pushed himself onto hands and knees, then stood up. "Who's there?" called a voice that Longarm recognized as belonging to Joe.

"It's me, Custis Long," he said. "Somebody get a lantern. We got trouble here."

A few moments later, a lucifer rasped into life and was held to the wick of a lantern carried by Pete. As the wick caught and the glow from the flame spread into a yellow circle on the deck, Longarm saw that the man lying at his

feet, out cold from the pistol barrel to the head, was a stranger.

Well, not completely, Longarm thought a second later as he studied the man's face. It was familiar somehow.

He realized why when Kate pushed her way through the cluster of men and said impatiently, "What's going on—good Lord! That's Carney Shaw. What happened to him?"

Longarm nodded to the unconscious man and asked Kate, "You know this fella?"

"Of course I do. He used to work for me."

"That's what I thought," Longarm said. "He was one of your old crew, wasn't he?"

"That's right." Kate was wearing a dressing gown, and her hair was tousled around her head from sleep. Longarm thought she looked softer, more vulnerable than usual because of it, and even more beautiful. "What's he doing here?"

Longarm holstered the Colt. "I reckon he snuck on board to bust up the wheel's driveshafts with an axe. He threw it at me when I surprised him."

"My God! You mean he was trying to sabotage the boat?"

"And he wasn't alone, either," Longarm said. "There was another fella with him. He jumped me back along the deck when I heard something odd and came to have a look-see. Tried to chop my head open with an axe. It's still stuck in the deck up yonder."

"I saw that," Kate said, an edge of horror in her voice. "Why would anybody . . ." Sharply indrawn breath hissed between her teeth. "McConnell."

Grantham and Swain had come up to join the crowd around Longarm, Kate, and the unconscious Carney Shaw. "Why would Mr. McConnell do such a thing?" Grantham asked. "He's already well ahead of us, isn't he?"

Longarm prodded Shaw in the shoulder with the toe of his boot. "Let's ask this gent here. Tim, fetch a water bucket."

Swain hurried off and came back a moment later with a bucket. "What do I do with it?" he asked.

Longarm pointed at Shaw. "Throw it in his face."

"Well . . . okay." Swain dumped the water from the bucket in Shaw's face.

Shaw came out of his stupor, sputtering and thrashing. Longarm knelt beside him, put a hand on Shaw's shoulder to force him back down, and jammed the barrel of the Colt under his jaw. "I ain't in a very good mood, old son," Longarm told him. "My head hurts like blazes, and I'm tired. So how about you tell us what you're doing here and whose idea it was."

Carney Shaw looked like a wall-eyed horse as he switched his gaze back and forth between the gun held so close to him and Longarm's grim face. With an effort, he swallowed and said, "You . . . you can go to hell!"

Longarm pressed the gun barrel harder into the soft flesh under Shaw's jawline. "That ain't the right answer. Not hardly."

"I . . . I ain't talkin'."

Longarm leaned closer to him and said quietly, "Listen to me, you son of a bitch. The hombre who was with you came too damned close to splittin' my head open. I don't like that. Then he jumped overboard and got away, left you here by your lonesome. Since he's gone and I can't get even with him, I may just have to take it out on you."

"Custis," Kate said. "Custis, I don't want you to hurt him. He used to be one of my crew—"

"And tonight he was about to ruin your boat," Longarm pointed out.

Kate didn't reply for a moment. Then she said coldly, "That's true. Do whatever you want to him."

Joe leaned forward. "Why don't you let me and my brothers have him, Mr. Long? We've got a score to settle with his bunch for shooting our pa."

"Whaaat?" Shaw exclaimed in a quavery voice. "We didn't shoot nobody, especially not that old redskin! Damn it, keep those boys away from me!"

Longarm withdrew his gun from Shaw's throat and smiled icily down at him. "Maybe that's a good idea. We'll let Joe and Pete and Carl talk to you."

120

"It was Ike's idea!" Shaw burst out. He sat up, and this time Longarm let him. "He said if a couple of us got on board with axes and busted up your shafts and gears, you'd never even make it to Circle City!"

"Why would Carpen want to ruin my boat?" Kate asked. "You've already beaten us."

Shaw shook his head. "We had a valve blow out a couple of hours after we passed you. The boat's tied up no more'n a mile or two on upriver, while Ben tries to fix it."

Kate stiffened. "What? You mean McConnell's not miles ahead?" Her hand shot out and gripped Longarm's arm. "We can get ahead again! It's not over!"

Longarm felt some of the same excitement that was washing over Kate, but his reaction was tempered by caution. "If McConnell don't have his boat ready to go by morning, then maybe—"

"Morning, hell! We're shoving off again *tonight*!" She turned to Joe, Pete, and Carl. "You boys go down to the engine room and start getting up some steam. Thank God we got the fireboxes filled!"

"Kate—Cap'n—hang on a minute," Longarm said. "It's dangerous running the river at night—"

She whipped around toward him. "I know the Yukon better than anyone!" she blazed. "We can do it, Custis, I know we can! We'll get so far ahead of McConnell he'll never catch up!"

In the lanternlight, her face was full of life and color and hope. Longarm remembered the despair that had filled her eyes earlier in the day when the *Katie* had passed them and she'd been forced to give up rather than risk blowing the boilers. Now that a chance to win had been dangled in front of her eyes, Longarm couldn't ruthlessly snatch it away from her.

He sighed and said, "All right, we'll give it a shot."

Kate was a ball of fire then, parceling out the chores that had to be done before they could shove off, alerting the passengers to what was going on, and then climbing to the wheelhouse in her nightclothes. Once she was gone, Long-

arm hauled Carney Shaw to his feet and said quietly to him, "I got another question or two for you, old son."

"What is it?" Shaw asked, his voice surly.

"How'd you get down here, and who came with you?"

"We had a little skiff. It wasn't any problem to let the current carry us down along that bluff on the other side of the river, where nobody could see us because of the shadows."

"You and who else?" Longarm prodded.

"Ike," Shaw answered reluctantly.

So it had been Carpen who nearly split his head open like a melon, Longarm thought. Somehow, that didn't surprise him.

"One more thing: did McConnell know what the two of you were up to?"

"I don't know. I really don't, mister. Ike's the one who gave the orders. Ben was working on that valve when we left, so he might not have known."

Longarm nodded slowly. He would have been willing to bet that the sabotage attempt had been Carpen's idea instead of McConnell's. Right from the start, Carpen had struck him as the more dangerous of the two.

"Carpen's the one who took that potshot at the boat this afternoon, too, right?"

"Yeah. Ben gave him hell for it."

"Gonna have to lock you in the storeroom, old son," Longarm told Shaw. "Can't have you running around loose tonight. But if you want, we'll let you go when we pass the *Katie*. If you want to try to swim back over to her, that's all right with me."

"I'm obliged," Shaw said. His teeth were starting to chatter as the night grew colder. "You reckon I could have a blanket or something? I'm wet, and that makes the air awful chilly."

Longarm thought about the way Shaw had thrown that axe at him and was tempted to tell the man to go to hell and warm up there, but he decided that wouldn't really serve any purpose. "We'll rustle you up a blanket," he said. "But next

time you better think about that before you come sneakin'
around."

"There won't be a next time," Shaw vowed. "From here
on out, Ike Carpen can handle his own skullduggery as far
as I'm concerned."

"Now you're gettin' smart," Longarm grinned. "Let's go."

He got a blanket from his own cabin for Shaw, then locked
the man into the storeroom off the galley. Muleshoe was
there, already brewing a pot of coffee, and Longarm told him
in a voice loud enough for Shaw to hear through the door,
"If that gent raises a ruckus or gives you any trouble, Muleshoe, just haul out that Dragoon of yours and blast a few
shots through the door."

"I durned sure will," Muleshoe replied, also loud enough
for Shaw to hear.

Longarm didn't think the fella would give any more trouble.

He climbed to the wheelhouse and found Kate there, charts
out on the table. She was bending over them, and the robe
she wore was open a little at the throat, revealing a smooth
expanse of creamy skin. She glanced up at Longarm and said,
"We can make it, Custis, I know we can. There aren't any
sandbars or bad snags up ahead for a good long way."

"That you know of," Longarm said. "Rivers can change."
He saw the top of the valley between her breasts and found
it intriguing.

She straightened and pulled the robe tighter around her,
cinching its belt. "We're going upriver," she said, a touch of
defiance in her voice.

"You're the cap'n," Longarm told her.

"That's right, I am." She turned to the speaking tube,
grasped it, and said, "How's the steam coming along, Joe?"

"Ready in another fifteen minutes or so," came the muffled
reply through the rubber tube.

"Let me know," Kate told him, then turned back to Longarm. "It's obvious now that McConnell won't stop at anything to beat me. When we pass his boat, I want you to have

your rifle ready, Custis. If they want a war, then by God we'll give it to them!"

Longarm thought of what Shaw had told him about Carpen and how McConnell might not have even known about the attempt to sabotage the *Yukon Queen*. It would just muddle things to go into that with Kate now, and besides, she wasn't in any mood to hear it. He just nodded his agreement with her order.

Losing a boat race was one thing, losing a shooting war was another. Longarm didn't intend to come out on the short end of *that* stick.

They shoved off at two in the morning. In another hour or so it would be the dawn of another unnaturally long Alaskan summer day. Running the river for an hour of darkness wasn't taking too big a chance, Longarm told himself, especially since Kate knew the Yukon so well. But he would keep his fingers crossed anyway that they wouldn't encounter some unexpected trouble.

The men on board the *Katie* must have heard the *Yukon Queen* coming, because as the boat rounded a bend in the river and came in sight of the other vessel, Longarm saw quite a few figures lined up at the railing. He stood on the bow with the Winchester in his hands. Joe was posted at the stern, also carrying a rifle. Down below, Pete, Carl, and the two youngsters from back East manned the engines and the boilers. Kate was at the wheel.

Longarm was ready to duck behind the capstan and use it for cover if any shots came from the other boat. None did, however. An air of glumness hung over the *Katie* as the *Yukon Queen* slid smoothly past it.

Shaw, the saboteur Longarm had captured the night before, clambered over the rail and dropped into the river. He started swimming toward the *Katie*.

Longarm moved closer to the rail and looked back as McConnell's boat fell behind. He couldn't help but grin. McConnell had pushed his vessel too hard, and that carelessness had caught up with him. If he got the valve repaired,

he probably wouldn't be able to risk running the engines full-out again, not if he wanted to reach Circle City.

The Yukon curved again, and the other boat disappeared around that bend. The *Yukon Queen* steamed on, running fast and free.

By daylight, Muleshoe had breakfast ready, and the crew took turns eating. Kate refused to leave the wheelhouse, so Longarm took a plate up to her and relieved her at the wheel while she ate. The country was prettier than ever. They were among the mountains now, stony gray peaks topped with snow and ice that loomed over the deep green of the pine and spruce and cedar forests covering the valley along the river.

"I can see why you like it up here," Longarm commented as he stood with his hands on the wheel. "Mighty pretty scenery."

"It's not like this in the winter," Kate said. She sipped from a cup of coffee. "Then it's just snow and ice as far as the eye can see. But I've never seen a more beautiful place during the summer."

"And there's gold to boot," Longarm mused. "Some folks still call this Seward's Folly."

"They just don't know what they're missing," Kate said.

The wheelhouse door was open. Longarm tensed as he heard his name being called from down on deck somewhere. "Mr. Long! Mr. Long!"

"Sounds like Raymond," he said as he turned from the wheel. Kate moved to take his place.

"See what's wrong," she told him anxiously. "I don't like the sound of that."

Neither did Longarm. He stepped out onto the upper deck that formed the roof of the cabins and leaned over to see Raymond Grantham standing near the stern. Grantham had his right hand cupped around his mouth, but his left was pointing back downriver.

Longarm saw right away what the boy was pointing at. A riverboat had come into sight behind them, chugging steadily along the Yukon with smoke boiling from its stack.

Longarm bit back a curse as he recognized the other vessel. He waved to Grantham to indicate that he had seen the boat, then went back into the wheelhouse.

"What is it?" Kate asked. "Bad news, I'll bet."

"McConnell's back," Longarm told her. "He's about three hundred yards behind us."

Kate didn't say anything, but Longarm saw her hands clench more tightly on the wheel. She kept her eyes fixed on the river up ahead for a long moment, then asked, "Are you sure? There's a spyglass in the chart table if you need it."

"I'm sure," Longarm told her. "There's nobody else coming this way in a riverboat."

"No," Kate agreed softly. She sighed. "He must've gotten that valve repaired not long after we passed him."

Longarm took out a cheroot and put it in his mouth to chew on it. "I don't know much about boat engines," he said around the tightly rolled cylinder of tobacco, "but I figure once you've blown out a valve, you can't put as much of a strain on it as you did before."

"That's right," Kate said. "He can't push his engines like he did during the first part of the trip. If we'd only had a day or two to build up a lead, he wouldn't have caught us before we got to Circle City."

"What about now? We're only running at half speed."

Kate glanced back at him and smiled. "You sound like you really want to win, Custis. I didn't think this race meant all that much to you, that you were just using it as a way to get to Circle City."

"I don't cotton to the idea of somebody swinging an axe at my head," Longarm said, his teeth clenching on the cheroot. "What say we go to three-quarters?"

"Give the order, first mate."

Longarm grabbed the speaking tube and called into it, "Hey, Joe! Ahead three-quarters!"

"Ahead three-quarters!" Joe responded, and a moment later Longarm felt and heard an increase in the thrumming from the engines.

"If there was enough damage to that valve, maybe we can

still stay ahead of McConnell," Kate said as she concentrated on the river. "It'll mean running neck and neck all the way to Circle City and not stopping for anything unless we have to take on wood."

"Is there enough in the boxes to get us there?"

Kate shook her head. "I just don't know. We'll have to wait and see."

Longarm took the spyglass Kate had mentioned from the chart table and lifted it to his eye as he looked back along the river. The *Katie* sprang into sharp focus through the lens. He saw men standing on her bow, but none of them seemed to be armed, which was a relief. Running a race like this was hard enough without making a gun battle of it. He raised the glass to the other boat's wheelhouse and saw both McConnell and Carpen. McConnell was at the wheel. Even with the spyglass, the distance was too great to make out the redhead's expression, but he seemed to be gripping the wheel tightly, with an air of tension hanging over him.

"Are they getting closer?" Kate asked.

"If they are, it ain't by much."

That was the way it went for the next several hours. The *Yukon Queen* maintained its slim lead on the *Katie*, but as the sun reached its zenith and slid over into afternoon, Longarm had to admit that McConnell's boat was closing the gap.

Even an occasional glance back was enough to tell Kate the same thing. She beat a fist against the wheel and said, "Damn it, not again!"

"That boat doesn't have the speed that it did before, but it's still faster'n ours unless we go all out," Longarm said. "We can't do that, Kate."

"I know it." Her voice was filled with despair. "I thought we had a chance again, Custis, I really did."

"So did I," he agreed. "I guess it just wasn't in the cards."

By mid-afternoon, despite the best efforts of everyone on the *Yukon Queen*, the *Katie* was pulling abreast. This time the boat passed them on the port side, with McConnell's passengers and crew whooping in delight and derision. Kate stood at the wheel and stared stonily ahead, refusing to as

much as glance over at the other vessel as it pulled even and then ahead.

The boats were close enough so that Longarm could see the grin on McConnell's face as the redhead stood at the wheel. He didn't see Carpen anywhere now, which was sort of worrisome. He hoped the son of a bitch wasn't getting up to some more deviltry.

The *Katie* passed the *Yukon Queen* and steamed on up the river, gradually drawing away. It was a couple of hundred yards ahead as the river rounded yet another bend and then narrowed to run in a straightaway through a cut between two beetling bluffs. The *Katie* was just about to enter the cut when Kate suddenly said, "What the hell is that?"

Longarm stepped up beside her and saw a lot of long, dark shapes floating on the river toward the *Katie*. The boat abruptly changed course, angling toward the far side of the river as McConnell must have spun the wheel, but his reaction had come too late, and anyway, there were too many of the obstacles.

"Logs!" Kate exclaimed. "Those are logs!"

Longarm saw that she was right—the objects barreling down on the *Katie*, carried by the swift current of the Yukon, were long, thick, heavy logs. It was impossible for McConnell to avoid all of them, and as Longarm and Kate watched, several of the logs smashed into the bow of the riverboat.

Kate suddenly spun the wheel of the *Yukon Queen*. "We have to get closer to shore!" she cried. "The ones that miss McConnell are coming at us! All ahead full!"

Longarm saw she was right. They had to risk asking the engines to give all they could, or the logs might wreck the *Yukon Queen*, too. He grabbed the speaking tube and shouted to Joe, "All ahead full!"

The engines roared and the steamboat leaped ahead, veering hard to starboard. The current was the strongest in the center of the river, so that's where most of the logs were. If Kate could get the boat close to shore in time, the logs might miss them.

Longarm didn't have to ask where the logs had come from. He saw flashes on the bluffs overlooking the river and knew they were muzzle flashes from rifles in the hands of men perched up there. He remembered what Grover Hanratty had said about a gang of river pirates working the upper stretches of the Yukon.

The pirates had picked a good spot for their ambush. The narrowness of the river where it entered the cut between the bluffs meant that McConnell hadn't really had anyplace to run once he spotted the logs bearing down on him. And the high ground on both sides of the river allowed the pirates to pour gunfire down onto the boat.

As Longarm watched, the *Katie* began to list to port. Kate saw it, too. "Her hull is holed!" she said. "They're going down!"

And unless they got out of the way of those logs, the same fate awaited the *Yukon Queen*.

Chapter 11

The range was still pretty far, but Longarm snatched up the Winchester he'd leaned in the corner of the wheelhouse and started firing at the bluffs up ahead. He knew it would be sheer luck if he actually hit any of the pirates, but maybe he could at least make them duck a little.

Besides, there was nothing he could do now to help Kate. Saving the *Yukon Queen* from the vicious trap was entirely in her hands.

The riverboat swung closer and closer to shore. The first of the logs that had missed the *Katie* slid past, missing the *Yukon Queen* by no more than fifteen feet. From the wheelhouse, Longarm saw that its ends had been whittled down to points by axes so that it would be more likely to penetrate the hull of any boat it crashed into. The next log actually struck the boat, but at such an angle that it glanced off rather than smashing a hole through the hull. Still, Longarm winced as he felt the impact.

The rifle was empty by now. He took a box of shells from his coat pocket and began reloading. As he did so, he saw that the *Katie* was in really bad shape, riding at such an angle in the water that walking the deck would have been nearly impossible. No one was trying to do that, however. Instead, the passengers and crew were abandoning the boat, leaping off into the river before it could sink completely.

As it was the rest of its length, the Yukon was cold and swift-running along here, with the current perhaps even a little faster than usual because the river narrowed down to pass between the bluffs. Longarm heard men screaming and yelling and knew that some of them probably would be pulled under the surface, never to come up again. Not only that, but the pirates were still peppering the river with rifle fire.

The *Yukon Queen* was close to the riverbank now. It had been struck by only one log, and most of the rest had already floated past. Longarm finished reloading the Winchester and levered a shell into the chamber as Kate spun the wheel once more, this time hard to port. She was heading back out into the center of the river.

"What are you doing?" Longarm shouted at her over the roar of the laboring engines.

"We've got to get those men out of the water!"

He nodded grimly in understanding. "Then you're going to run that cut between the bluffs?"

Kate glanced at him, her eyes full of a mixture of fear, anger, and determination. "If we put in to shore and tie up, we'll be sitting ducks for those damned pirates!"

Longarm hefted the rifle and grinned at her. "Let's go, then!"

Making a run for it like this wasn't quite as foolhardy as it seemed, he thought. Chances were the gang of pirates didn't have any other traps prepared. They wouldn't have been expecting two riverboats to come along so close together. Now that the *Yukon Queen* had avoided the danger of the floating logs, all that remained was to run the gauntlet between the bluffs.

Longarm stepped out of the wheelhouse. Everybody on board had felt the lurch as the boat changed course and was aware that the engines were running full speed now. They knew that something was going on, and those who were on deck had no doubt seen the wrecking of the *Katie*. Longarm cupped a hand around his mouth and yelled, "Hunt some cover! If you've got guns, get ready for a fight!"

Yak came up the ladder from the deck, climbing awkwardly because his left arm was in a sling. "Gimme a gun," he said to Longarm. "I can shoot."

Joe swarmed up the ladder after his father, a pair of rifles tucked under his arm. Longarm gestured toward the young man and said to Yak, "You can do more good loading for your boy there. Those are single-shot rifles."

For a second Yak looked like he wanted to argue, but then he nodded. He and Joe went into the wheelhouse together.

Longarm ran along the roof of the cabins to the stern. The paddlewheel was turning smoothly. If the engines held up, they would have plenty of speed going through the cut. The passengers on deck were crowding behind every bit of cover they could find. Longarm didn't much like it, but they would just have to take their chances.

He went down the ladder at the rear of the cabins, then ran forward again. Raymond Grantham and Timothy Swain emerged from the hatch leading belowdecks just as Longarm passed it, so he said to them, "Come on up to the bow!"

The two young men seemed cool-headed despite the fact that they were about to be under fire. They followed Longarm to the bow. "Grab those poles we use to shove off," he ordered them, "and get ready to fish out as many of the survivors as you can. I'll cover you."

They picked up the long poles and moved to the port side, where men from the *Katie* were floundering in the river. The current was sweeping them toward the *Yukon Queen*. Some of them came close enough they were able to leap up and grab the gunwale or even the railing. Others caught hold of the poles extended over the water by Grantham and Swain. The two young men braced themselves so they wouldn't be pulled overboard, too. Several passengers who saw what was going on left the meager shelter they had found and hurried forward to help. Within a matter of moments, men were being hauled dripping out of the frigid water to relative safety.

Longarm saw a bullet *plunk!* into the water not far from the bow. As the *Yukon Queen* passed the now almost completely submerged *Katie*, Longarm lifted the Winchester to

132

his shoulder and started firing. Instead of spraying the bluffs as he had done earlier, this time he fired slowly and deliberately, picking his targets by the puffs of smoke and the muzzle flashes from the bushwhackers' guns. The riverboat entered the cut between the bluffs, which Longarm estimated as eighty feet high. He pivoted from side to side as he fired, hoping to make the rats on both sides of the river hunt cover.

Joe was shooting from the wheelhouse, too, a steady fire but even slower than Longarm's because he was using the single-shot rifles. Still, after one blast from the wheelhouse, Longarm saw a figure topple from the top of the northern bluff and plummet into the river. Joe had drawn first blood. Elsewhere on the deck, some of the passengers who were armed were also bombarding the bluffs with gunfire.

When he had emptied the Winchester again, Longarm turned to Grantham and Swain and saw that they were still helping men onto the boat. Almost everyone was out of the water, though. In fact, only one man was still afloat in the river, as far as Longarm could see, and he was clutching a rope that someone had tossed him. He had been dragged into the cut behind the riverboat. A flash of bright red hair told Longarm that the man was Ben McConnell.

He set the rifle aside and hurried over to grasp the rope. He started tugging it in, ignoring the bullets that whined past from time to time. When McConnell was beside the boat, Longarm knelt and extended a hand to him. McConnell and Longarm clasped each other's wrists, and with a bunching of muscles in his arms and shoulders, Longarm hauled the redhead out of the river. McConnell caught hold of the railing with his free hand and helped pull himself up and over. Both he and Longarm sprawled onto the deck. McConnell's chest rose and fell rapidly as he tried to draw breath back into his body. He was blue-faced and shaking from the chill of being in the river for several minutes.

Seeing that McConnell was going to be all right, Longarm got to his feet and snatched up the Winchester again. He glanced at the bluffs. The riverboat was more than halfway through the cut by now, and not nearly as many shots were

coming from above. The pirates had been clustered at the other end. They were trying to pursue the boat along the bluffs, but the terrain was rugged up there, Longarm saw. He thumbed more cartridges into the Winchester and started shooting again. Might as well discourage the bastards as much as possible, he told himself.

Within minutes, the sternwheeler was through the cut. A few last slugs from the bluffs smacked harmlessly into the paddlewheel. The river widened out again, as did the valley on either side of it. Longarm ran along the deck to the stern, sweeping his gaze across this side of the bluffs, but he didn't see any pursuit. The pirates probably had horses, but evidently they weren't interested in giving chase to the boat that had escaped their trap.

He went back along the deck toward the bow and found McConnell sitting up with his back against a cabin wall. McConnell looked up at him and said in a voice hoarse from swallowing river water, "Thanks, Long."

"*De nada*. Come on." He helped McConnell to his feet. "The person you really ought to thank is up in the wheelhouse."

McConnell looked grim, but he nodded.

Longarm led the way, and when he and McConnell entered the wheelhouse a moment later, Kate turned to look at them with an expression of relief on her face. "Thank God!" she exclaimed. "I thought you might both be dead."

Yak and Joe both grinned at Longarm. Yak clapped Joe on the shoulder and said, "Boy shoot good."

"He sure does," Longarm agreed. To Kate, he said, "You reckon we better slow down now?"

She nodded. "Tell Pete to cut the engines back to one-half."

Longarm relayed the order while McConnell stood by looking cold and uncomfortable. The chill that gripped him wasn't the only source of his discomfort, however. He finally said, "Thanks for helping us, Kate."

"We're river people, Ben," she told him coolly. "We don't

134

stand by and watch each other drown if there's something we can do about it."

"Those damned pirates!" McConnell said. "I couldn't get the boat turned in time when I saw those logs coming at us."

"There wasn't time or room for that," Kate said. "It was a good trap." She paused, then added, "Sorry about the boat. And your passengers and crew. Did you lose very many?"

"I don't know yet." McConnell rubbed a hand wearily over his face. "I'd better go down and see how many got fished out. I hope not too many drowned." He looked at Longarm. "Did you see Ike down there on deck anywhere?"

Longarm shook his head. He had looked for Carpen, wanting to be aware of it if McConnell's treacherous first mate was now on board the *Yukon Queen*. He hadn't seen any sign of the man, however.

"Damn it," McConnell muttered. "This is all my fault."

"You didn't set that trap with the logs," Longarm told him. "That gang of pirates did that."

"But the men who died . . . they were there because of me."

"Ben . . ." Kate said. "It really wasn't your fault."

McConnell's expression was bleak as he drew in a deep breath. "One of these days I'll settle the score with those bastards," he vowed. "Until then . . . Kate, you'll take the rest of us on to Circle City?"

"Of course," she answered without hesitation. "The boat will be pretty crowded, but we'll manage."

"I'm much obliged," McConnell said. He laughed hollowly. "I guess the race really is over now, isn't it?"

Then he went to see just how many men had been lost when the *Katie* went down.

Like a half-drowned rat, Ike Carpen pulled himself out of the river and onto the bank. He flopped onto his belly, gasping for air and shaking with a terrible chill at the same time. It was hard for his stunned brain to comprehend that he actually had survived the wreck of the riverboat and the dunking in the icy Yukon.

The men on horseback had come up in a half-circle around him on the riverbank before he was even aware that they were there. When the sound of hooves shuffling around finally penetrated his brain, he looked up and saw the rough clothes, the fur caps, the hard, unshaven faces, and knew that these were the men who had set the log trap for the riverboat.

"Well, I'll be a ring-tailed son of a bitch," said one of the riders, a huge, black-bearded man in a coat made from the hide of a bear. "Howdy, Ike."

Carpen blinked at the river pirate. "Dixon? My G-God, is that you?"

The pirate called Dixon lowered the rifle he was holding in one hand until its muzzle was almost touching Carpen's forehead. Smiling, he said, "If there's any reason I shouldn't blow your brains out, Ike, you better tell me now."

Eight men from the *Katie*, including Ike Carpen, were missing and presumed drowned in the Yukon River. Everyone else had been rescued. Three of the dead men had been crew members, the other five were passengers. McConnell felt especially bad about losing those five. The members of the crew had been aware of the risks when they agreed to take the riverboat up the Yukon to the gold fields.

The atmosphere on board the *Yukon Queen* was pretty gloomy at first as the paddlewheeler proceeded on toward Circle City. As the days passed, however, the gold seekers began to look forward again to the fortunes they surely would make as soon as they arrived at their destination. The cramped conditions on board made for some friction, and there were a couple of minor ruckuses between the Argonauts, but overall the rest of the trip upriver went surprisingly well, with no further sign of the pirates. The *Yukon Queen* arrived at Circle City seventeen days after leaving St. Michael. That was making good time, Kate told Longarm.

Circle City, like St. Michael, was a crude settlement of log buildings, tents, and shacks that looked as if they would collapse in a stiff breeze. The saloon owners and the merchants were glad to see a new group of gold seekers, who went

seeking whiskey and supplies as soon as they disembarked from the *Yukon Queen*.

Longarm and Kate stood in the wheelhouse and watched the passengers leave, clomping down the gangplank and spreading out through the settlement. Kate leaned on the chart table and said, "I guess you'll be going out to make your fortune now, too, Custis."

Longarm shrugged. "I ain't in any hurry." In truth, he was anxious to start looking for Harrison Dodge, but at the same time he would miss Kate. "How long are you going to be here before you start back to St. Michael?"

"I don't know," she replied with a shake of her head. "It depends on how long it takes me to round up a full crew. Yak and his sons are staying on, but I don't know about Muleshoe. And I'll be losing you and those two college boys."

Longarm didn't tell her that if he was able to locate and arrest Harrison Dodge before the *Yukon Queen* headed downriver, he would be making the return voyage with her. That was exactly what he hoped would happen. He didn't want to be stuck here in Circle City waiting for the return of the other riverboat.

"I'm sure you'll be able to find some fellas who're willing to work," Longarm said.

Kate smiled regretfully as she stood up and moved closer to him. "I won't be able to find a first mate like you, Custis."

"Hell, I didn't do all that much—"

"You did enough." She was closer to him now, close enough so that she could reach up, put her arms around his neck, and draw his head down to hers. Their lips met, and Longarm felt the sudden heat that flowed between their bodies.

Kate's body molded to his, soft yet insistent, and Longarm's shaft began to harden. Kate had to be able to feel it as it rose and prodded into her belly. Her hips moved, pressing her loins against Longarm. The lower halves of their bodies ground together as they kissed. Longarm's tongue

slipped between Kate's eagerly opened lips and explored her mouth.

After a long, heated moment, she moved back enough so that she could reach between their bodies and caress his manhood through his trousers. Longarm's hands moved down her back to cup the cheeks of her rump as they molded the fabric of her tight trousers. Kate was the sort of woman who kept herself under strict control most of the time, Longarm sensed, but once she ever let herself go, she would be a skilled, inventive, demanding lover.

Someone cleared his throat from the door of the wheelhouse.

Kate broke the kiss, gasped, and practically leaped away from Longarm. "Ben!" she said as she looked at McConnell. "What do you want?"

Longarm turned and saw the former first mate of the *Yukon Queen* standing there. McConnell's rugged face was taut with anger, but he kept a tight rein on his emotions as he said, "I just thought I'd let you know that all the passengers are off the boat." From the way McConnell said the words, Longarm had the feeling this was one of the duties the redhead had performed when he worked for Kate.

"Thanks," Kate said. She was flushed and flustered from the kiss that had been interrupted.

McConnell started to turn away. "Guess I'll be going now, too."

"Ben—" Kate stopped him. "What are you going to do? Now that the other boat is . . . is . . ."

"Gone?" McConnell shrugged. "Maybe I can get somebody to grubstake me so that I can look for gold."

"You're not a prospector," Kate said. "You're a riverman. Come back to work for me."

McConnell's face hardened even more. He glanced at Longarm and said, "I don't think so. You've already got a . . . first mate."

"Not me," Longarm said. "I got to find the fella I came up here to look for."

"Please think about it, Ben," Kate said. "The other men can come back, too, if they want to."

"Some of 'em might . . . I'll ask around. But my riverboat days are over." With that, McConnell turned away and started down the ladder, and he didn't stop when Kate called his name once more.

Longarm looked at her and saw her hands clenching into fists. "That . . . that stubborn bastard!" she said. "Can't he see that it makes sense for him to come back?"

"A fella's common sense sometimes takes a backseat to his pride," Longarm said. "McConnell feels like he's busted all the way around now, since he lost that boat."

"That wasn't his fault."

"Nope, it wasn't," Longarm agreed. "It could've just as easily been us in the lead, and then we would've been sunk by that trap. But that ain't the way it worked out."

Kate's eyes searched his face. "I don't suppose it would do any good to ask you to talk to him . . . ?"

"He wouldn't listen to me any more than he would to you. Likely even less."

Kate's mouth thinned into a grim line. "All right, then. To hell with Ben McConnell. Maybe one of the other men would like to come back and be my first mate. If not, I'll offer the job to Joe."

"Might be your best bet," Longarm said. He stepped over to her and bent to kiss her on the forehead. "I got to be goin', Kate. Things to do, gents to see."

She looked up at him and whispered, "Good-bye, Custis. Good luck."

"To you, too."

He left her in the wheelhouse and went to get his gear. It wasn't easy, but he did it.

Longarm intended to make the nearest saloon in Circle City his first stop, but as he passed one of the general stores, he decided to go in there instead. The crudely lettered sign over the front door of the log building read TRUMAN'S STORE SUPPLIES—WHISKEY—GUNS

Everything a fella needed to go looking for gold, Longarm thought wryly.

He went inside and found several of the passengers from the *Yukon Queen* crowding around a counter, clamoring for supplies for their gold-hunting trips. One man was doing his best to wait on the crowd. He was small and nervous-looking, with a bristly mustache and thinning hair. He was slightly pop-eyed over a prominent nose.

"Hold your horses, hold your horses," he kept muttering. "Now, who's next?"

The proprietor could have used some help, Longarm thought, but the only other person inside the store besides the customers was a man in an oversized fur coat who had an equally ill-fitting fur cap pulled down over his head. He was using a broom to sweep along the aisles of the store between shelves full of provisions. Longarm glanced his way, then ignored him. He folded his arms and waited for the crowd at the counter in the rear of the store to clear out. He wanted to ask the harried-looking proprietor if he'd seen a man who fit the description of Harrison Dodge, but Longarm didn't think he'd get a straight answer as long as the store was so busy. To help curb his impatience, Longarm took out a cheroot and lit it.

As he puffed on the cigar, the hair on the back of his neck began to prickle. Longarm knew the feeling—someone was staring at him. All too often in his career as a lawman, that warning sensation had been followed closely by the icy feeling that some son of a bitch was drawing a bead on him with a gun. Longarm turned quickly, his hand dropping to his gun—

And saw that the person staring at him was the man who had been sweeping up. The gent's eyes were wide with recognition, as well as fright.

"Shit!" Longarm exclaimed around the cheroot. "Dodge!"

The bulky coat and the ridiculous cap had been enough to disguise Dodge, but only momentarily. Longarm lunged toward the fugitive. Dodge seemed frozen in his tracks for a

split-second, then he let out a yelp and threw the broom at Longarm.

The broom wouldn't have done much damage if it hadn't skittered between Longarm's feet and tripped him. He yelled a curse as he lost his balance and toppled sideways, falling into the shelves. A whole section of them went crashing over, prompting the storekeeper to shout angrily, "Hey! What the hell's goin' on there?"

Longarm scrambled to his feet as Harrison Dodge ducked through the front door and disappeared. A couple of long, running strides brought Longarm to the doorway. He peered right and left and spotted Dodge to the right, scurrying toward the river. The long coat flopped absurdly around his legs as he ran.

Dodge was still well within pistol range. Longarm could have hauled out his Colt and tried to wing the fugitive. He didn't want to take a chance on killing Dodge, however, so he had no choice except to break into a run after him.

Dodge threw a frantic glance over his shoulder as he fled. Men stared at him as he raced past them, but no one moved to stop him. Up here in Alaska Territory, as in all the rest of the earth's frontiers, men minded their own business.

Longarm's low-heeled boots pounded the hard-packed ground as he closed in on Dodge. Suddenly, coming toward them up ahead, he saw Raymond Grantham and Timothy Swain. The two youngsters stopped as they saw Longarm running toward them, obviously chasing a small figure in a flapping coat and funny-looking hat.

Within a matter of moments, Longarm would have caught Dodge anyway, but he decided that since Grantham and Swain were standing right there, they might as well make themselves useful. "Grab that little varmint!" he shouted to them, pointing at Dodge. "Stop him!"

Grantham and Swain hesitated, then threw themselves out in front of Dodge. Dodge tried to veer around them, but the two young men split up, blocking his path. With a cry of anger and frustration, Dodge swung his fist at Swain's head. Swain wasn't expecting the blow and didn't get out of the

way in time. Dodge's fist cracked against his jaw and knocked him backward. Swain tripped and fell.

Before Dodge could dart past the fallen Swain, Raymond Grantham tackled him. Grantham's arms wrapped around Dodge's thighs and spilled both men off their feet. Dodge howled a curse and kicked out at Grantham, freeing himself. As he tried to scramble to his feet, however, Longarm caught up to him, and the lawman's hand came down hard on his shoulder, shoving him face first to the ground.

Longarm knelt with his right knee in the small of Dodge's back. Remembering how Dodge had taken him by surprise in San Francisco, Longarm resolved not to take any chances with the fugitive this time, no matter how harmless and downright humorous Dodge might appear. He reached inside his coat, took out the pair of handcuffs he'd been carrying all the way from Denver, and yanked Dodge's left arm behind his back. Longarm snapped one of the cuffs onto Dodge's wrist, then grabbed Dodge's other arm. A second later, both of Dodge's hands were cuffed behind his back.

"Don't reckon you'll be trying any tricks this time, old son," Longarm said. "By the way, just to make it legal, you're under arrest." He turned his head to thank Grantham and Swain for giving him a hand with the capture—

Only to find Raymond Grantham staring coldly at him over the barrel of a pistol, which was lined up right between Longarm's eyes. "Please don't move, Marshal," the young man said. "After all this time, I'd hate to have to kill you."

Chapter 12

Longarm stared into the muzzle of the gun for a second, reflecting on how even a small caliber pistol could look damned near as big as a cannon when it was pointed at a fella's face. Then he said heavily, "You ain't a college boy at all, are you, Raymond? You work for the sons of bitches back in Washington who want Dodge dead."

Grantham didn't really answer the question. Instead, he said, "I didn't expect you to find him so quickly, Marshal. You've been quite lucky in this whole affair."

"Yeah," Longarm said, bitterly. "Lucky."

Swain climbed hurriedly to his feet and drew a revolver from underneath his coat. "I've got this little bastard covered," he said as he pointed the gun at the handcuffed Dodge, who lay face down on the ground and whimpered.

"All this way," Dodge said, as much to himself as to anyone else. "I come all this way, and they still catch me."

"Some people just aren't cut out to be fugitives," Grantham told him. "You should have thought of that before you threatened the man we work for."

"I didn't tell anybody anything!" Dodge wailed. "I don't *want* to testify! For God's sake, I was trying to get away!" A wheedling tone came into his voice as he lifted his head as best he could to peer imploringly at Grantham and Swain.

"Can't you just let me go and tell him you couldn't find me? I'll never be any threat to him, I swear!"

"What about the marshal here?"

"Kill him!" Dodge said viciously. "Just go ahead and kill him. Get it over with, damn it!"

"Well, if I ever felt kindly toward you, old son," Longarm said, "that just about took care of it."

He was stalling, talking in the hope that Grantham wouldn't pull the trigger while he was doing so. That was a pretty slim chance, though, judging by the cold glare of Grantham's eyes. It was amazing how with the guns in their hands, Grantham and Swain didn't look nearly as young and innocent as they had only minutes earlier.

A lot of men were standing around watching now, although once the guns had come out, the bystanders pulled back to give Grantham and Swain plenty of room. No one seemed to be about to interfere with them, Longarm judged as he glanced around. These men believed in tending to their own affairs and no one else's, a belief that was reinforced by the waving around of firearms.

"Damn it, I'm a federal marshal," Longarm snapped in disgust. "Are you gents going to just stand around while these two buzzards murder me and my prisoner?"

No one in the crowd budged, and after a moment Grantham smiled thinly. "It doesn't look like anyone is going to come to your rescue, Marshal."

The blast of a gun split the air just as the last derisive word left Grantham's mouth. Swain was thrown forward by the impact of a bullet striking him from behind. Involuntarily, Grantham twisted in that direction, and Longarm seized the chance to throw himself into a dive from his kneeling position. His shoulder slammed into Grantham's legs. Grantham's pistol cracked, and a fiery finger traced a path along Longarm's back.

He threw a looping punch that sank into Grantham's belly as the young man was falling. Longarm rolled over and surged to his feet. Swain was on his knees nearby, facing away from Longarm, his left arm hanging useless from his

shoulder but his right hand trying to reach the gun he had dropped when he was shot. Longarm knew that Swain intended to execute Dodge, who lay screaming in terror. He kicked Swain, his boot catching the would-be assassin between the shoulder blades and driving him forward.

Longarm spun around then, his hand slapping at the holster hanging from the cross-draw rig. It was empty. The Colt had slipped out when he'd tackled Grantham.

At the moment, however, Grantham had his hands full with Ben McConnell. McConnell had grabbed the young man and was shaking him like a terrier shakes a rat. Longarm didn't know where McConnell had come from, or if the big redhead had fired the shot that had wounded Swain, but he was grateful that McConnell was distracting Grantham. That gave Longarm a chance to scoop up his .45 from the ground and swing back around toward Swain.

"Hold it!" Longarm ordered as Swain reached once again for the gun he'd dropped. Longarm fired when Swain didn't stop. The slug hit the fallen pistol and kicked it away from Swain's outstretched fingers, smashing the cylinder at the same time. Swain froze, motionless in his awkward position.

McConnell drew back a fist and slammed it into Grantham's face, then hit him again. When McConnell let go of Grantham's collar, the young man collapsed in a senseless heap.

McConnell swung around toward Longarm, who was still covering Swain. "What the devil is this all about?" he demanded. "Did I hear one of these whelps call you 'Marshal'?"

"That's right," Longarm said. "I'm Deputy Marshal Custis Long, McConnell."

"You're not up here after gold?"

"Nope." Longarm nudged a booted toe into Dodge's ribs and went on, "Hush up that caterwauling." To McConnell, he said, "This fella right here is what I came up here after."

"He must be important."

"Important enough. I'm much obliged to you for taking a

145

hand. These boys were about ready to start shooting when you beat them to it."

McConnell shook his head as Dodge's cries died away to a whimper. "I didn't shoot," McConnell said. "I just jumped in after I saw what was going on."

Longarm frowned. "Then who . . . ?"

Joe shouldered through the crowd, one of the single-shot rifles under his arm. He grinned at Longarm and said, "Sorry I was almost a mite late."

McConnell grunted. "Let me guess—this redskin is a deputy marshal, too."

"Nope," Longarm replied with a grin, "just a friend. But with shootin' like that, if he wants to apply for a job carrying one of Uncle Sam's badges, I'll put in a good word for him."

"I'm no lawman," Joe said with a laugh. "I like working on the river better than fishing, though."

"From the way Cap'n Ridgway was talking earlier, you've got a job on the *Yukon Queen* for as long as you want it," Longarm told him. Joe nodded in satisfaction.

Longarm turned his attention to the problem of what to do with Grantham and Swain. Keeping his gun out, he reached down with his other hand, grasped Dodge's arm, and pulled the fugitive to his feet. "You all right?" he asked.

Dodge's nose was running, and the funny-looking fur cap had been knocked askew on his head. He sniffed and said, "I'm not hurt. But you can't take me back, you just can't. They'll kill me!"

"Not these two," Longarm said, nodding toward Grantham and Swain. Grantham was still only half-conscious, lying where he had fallen after McConnell punched him, while Swain had pulled himself into a sitting position and was cradling his injured arm. From the looks of the bloodstain on his sleeve, the bullet from Joe's rifle had ripped through the fleshy part of his upper arm.

Longarm looked around at the crowd and raised his voice to say, "In case any of you folks didn't hear, I'm a federal lawman, and this fella is my prisoner. These other two are

gunmen who were hired to kill him. I need a place to lock them up for a while."

The owner of the store where Dodge had been working pushed his way through the crowd. "My place has a good stout storeroom with a door that locks," he said. "You can put them there, Marshal."

Longarm nodded. "Much obliged, Mister . . . ?"

"Truman, Bert Truman." His thin chest swelled like a banty rooster's. Clearly, he was proud to be lending a hand to the law.

Swain looked up at Longarm and said miserably, "I need a doctor."

"I'll see that that bullethole gets patched up," Longarm promised, which he thought was more generous than Swain deserved. "Get on your feet. I reckon you're hurt too bad to carry your partner down to Mr. Truman's store, ain't you?"

Swain struggled to stand. "I'm a wounded man," he protested. "I can't carry anybody."

Several of the Argonauts who had come to Circle City on the *Yukon Queen* stepped forward. "We'll tote this no-good bastard for you, Marshal," one of them said.

Another man pointed at Dodge and asked, "What'd this little rapscallion do? He don't look like much of a criminal."

"That's between him and the law," Longarm answered. "My job is just to bring him back to answer to the authorities."

"These handcuffs hurt," Dodge sniveled. "Do they have to be so tight?"

"Keep talkin', old son," Longarm warned him, "and I'm liable to make 'em tighter. After what happened back in San Francisco, I ain't overly trustin' of you. Which same reminds me—what the hell did you hit me with in that hotel corridor?"

"A sap," Dodge admitted after a moment. "I made it myself when I left Washington. For protection. I . . . I don't really know how to handle a gun." A faint sneer touched his lips. "I figured most people would take one look at me and

147

decide that I wasn't dangerous, and you didn't let me down, Marshal."

Longarm thought about clenching his jaw and looking ferocious at Dodge, but then the absurdity of it struck him and he chuckled. "I reckon you're right about that," he admitted, and Dodge looked surprised.

Longarm herded Dodge in front of him down the street toward Truman's Store while several of the prospectors picked up Grantham's unconscious form and carried him. Swain was prodded along in the procession by McConnell and Joe.

"I got to go see Kate," Longarm commented to McConnell once the prisoners were safely locked up behind the sturdy door of Bert Truman's storeroom. "The *Yukon Queen* is the quickest way back to St. Michael, and the sooner I get there, the sooner I get back to Denver with my prisoner."

"You plan to commandeer her riverboat?" McConnell asked.

"Well . . . not unless I have to. If there are folks here in Circle City who want to book passage back to St. Michael, I reckon she ought to be able to carry 'em. But if she does wind up losing money, I'll do my best to see that she gets it back from Uncle Sam."

McConnell rubbed his jaw and frowned in thought as he stood there on the front porch of Truman's store along with Longarm, Joe, and the handcuffed Harrison Dodge. "I don't know if Kate still wants me back as first mate . . ." he mused.

"I reckon she wouldn't mind," Longarm said.

"I might be willing to make one more trip . . . just in case there's any more trouble."

Longarm told him, "I know I'd be glad to have you along." He inclined his head toward the store. "Those two are probably the only fellas in the whole territory who're after Dodge, but just in case they're not, it'd be good to have another fighting man around."

McConnell frowned again. "I don't want Kate thinking that she was right about everything."

Longarm grinned and said, "That'd need working out be-

tween you and her. It don't fall under federal jurisdiction."

McConnell took a deep breath and blew it out. "Well, let's go talk to her, I reckon. What can it hurt?"

"What the hell are you two cooking up?" Kate demanded suspiciously.

"Nothing," Longarm replied. "I just want you to head on back to St. Michael as soon as you can, and McConnell here says he'll be first mate for the trip."

Kate looked from one to the other of them and back again. She glared at Longarm and said, "I don't like being lied to."

"I ain't lying, Kate. I told you the truth just now."

"But not before," she accused. "You let me think you were just a prospector, when you're really a federal marshal."

"Deputy marshal," Longarm corrected mildly.

"All right, then, deputy marshal. And now you tell me you've got a prisoner down below that Joe's watching, and you have to get him back to civilization as soon as you can. Is that the reason you came up here to Alaska in the first place?"

Longarm nodded. "That's right."

"So coming with me like you did . . . it was just a job to you?"

Warning bells sounded in Longarm's brain again. He had a feeling he was about to be bushwhacked.

"Well . . . I really did want to help you out . . . and I figured if I rounded up a crew for you, that'd be the quickest way for me to get back on Dodge's trail . . ."

Judging by the storm clouds gathering in Kate's eyes, he wasn't doing himself any good. Might as well just shut up and quit digging the hole any deeper, he thought.

"All right," Kate said. "I'll take you back to St. Michael. We can't leave any earlier than first thing in the morning, though. It'll take that long to refill the fireboxes. I wouldn't mind picking up a few supplies from Bert Truman, too, even though his prices are close to outright thievery."

Longarm smiled at her. "I thank you, Kate," he said, "and the United States Justice Department thanks you."

149

"The United States Justice Department can damned well pay me. I'm going to submit a bill for transporting a federal prisoner."

"And I'll do my durnedest to see that it gets paid."

"It had better," she said ominously.

Sensing that now would be a good time to leave, Longarm said thanks again and stepped out of the wheelhouse. McConnell followed him down the ladder. When they both reached the main deck, McConnell gave Longarm a cocky grin and said, "I don't think Kate's going to be giving you any more kisses, Long." His expression grew more serious as he went on, "Anyway, she'd better not. And you'd be well advised to stay away from her."

Longarm asked coolly, "You tellin' me that on her account—or yours?"

"You may have fished me out of the river, but I settled that score when I tackled Grantham. Now we're even, and I'm telling you to stay away from Kate."

Longarm bristled instinctively at such a direct challenge, but he knew that what McConnell was saying made sense. Kate was mad at him for lying to her about who he really was and why he had come to Alaska, and now that he and McConnell had declared a truce of sorts, he didn't want to make an enemy out of the man once again.

Besides, he had a hunch that McConnell had some true feelings for Kate, even though he might be too prideful to show them. And several times, Longarm had sensed that Kate had a soft spot for the big redhead. Maybe it would be better all around if he just kept his distance, the way McConnell wanted. McConnell and Kate were both stubborn as jackasses, so maybe they deserved each other.

He chuckled, obviously taking McConnell by surprise. "Good luck, old son," Longarm said. "I reckon you may need it."

Longarm gave Bert Truman a double eagle in exchange for the storekeeper's promise to keep Grantham and Swain locked up for a week after the riverboat left for St. Michael.

150

It went against the grain for Longarm not to see that the two would-be assassins were brought to justice, but since there was no real law here in this part of the Alaska Territory and since he sure as blazes didn't want to be saddled with the two of them on the journey back downriver, he didn't have a whole lot of choice in the matter.

Of course, he reflected, he could just shoot both of them, but that seemed a mite extreme.

With a week's head start, there was no way Grantham and Swain could catch up to the *Yukon Queen*. They would have to either get hold of some horses or wait until the *Samuel Jennings* docked again in Circle City. By the time they finally reached the port at St. Michael, Longarm intended to be well on his way back to San Francisco with Dodge. Ships ran regularly along the Pacific coast between California and Alaska.

Early the next morning, the *Yukon Queen* was ready to shove off. Kate had only a dozen passengers, which meant that the crew outnumbered them this time. Besides McConnell, several other members of the old crew had asked for their jobs back.

Under the circumstances, Longarm made Joe a temporary deputy and gave him the responsibility for guarding Dodge whenever Longarm wasn't around. As the *Yukon Queen* left Circle City, Dodge was tied securely into a chair in Longarm's cabin, with Joe sitting nearby, a scattergun across his lap.

Longarm went out on deck to watch as the riverboat was pushed away from the dock. The engines were rumbling with a steady, deep-throated throb. The planks of the deck vibrated slightly under Longarm's feet. He stood with his hands on the railing as the paddlewheel revolved and sent the boat downriver. The engines wouldn't have to work nearly as hard on the return trip, since the boat would be going with the current instead of against it. The *Yukon Queen* began to pick up speed, and Circle City fell steadily behind.

A month and a half or thereabouts, and he'd be back in San Francisco with Dodge, Longarm reflected. From there,

a train ride to Denver, or maybe all the way to Washington if Billy Vail gave him the job of sticking with Dodge until the little man had testified. Then this case would be over.

It had had its pleasurable moments, Longarm thought, but by and large, the sooner he was finished with it, the better. He was ready to be someplace *warm* again.

A key rattled in a lock, and the door of the sturdy storage room in the back of Bert Truman's business swung open. Grantham and Swain were sitting on full sacks of flour. Grantham's face was bruised and swollen from Ben McConnell's fist, and Swain had his left arm bandaged and suspended in a crude sling. Both of them looked up in surprise as Truman moved into the doorway. The storekeeper was carrying a long-barreled pistol.

"My God, you're going to kill us, aren't you?" Grantham said in a hollow voice. "Long paid you to get rid of us."

Truman laughed. "Marshal Long paid me, all right, but just to hang on to you boys for a few days. And this is all he paid me." Truman reached in his pocket with his free hand and brought out a double eagle. He sneered at the coin and went on, "I figure it's worth a whole lot more to you fellas for me to let you out."

Grantham and Swain both stood up eagerly. "Whatever you want," Swain promised. "We can get the money."

Truman lifted the gun just in case they rushed him. "It ain't quite that easy," he said. "I don't know what that little fella Dodge did, but somebody wants him dead a whole heap. My partners and I can make that happen, but you got to cut us in for a share of the payoff."

"Partners?" Grantham repeated with a suspicious frown.

Truman came farther into the storeroom, and a big, bearded man in a bearskin coat bulked in the doorway behind him. "This is Breed Dixon," Truman said. "We got us a business arrangement. He takes supplies off the boats coming this direction and brings 'em to me, and I sell them back to the folks who lost them."

"Damn!" Swain exclaimed. "You're one of those river pirates!"

Dixon nodded as he came into the storeroom. A third and final man followed him. Truman grinned and said to Grantham and Swain, "I think you boys may know this gent. He's one of Breed's old pards, and he's part of the gang now."

Ike Carpen, dressed now in a coat and fur cap like Dixon, grinned at the two young men. "Howdy, boys," he said. "Surprised to see me?"

Chapter 13

Longarm moved along the deck in the moonlight. There was an extra chill in the air tonight, a harbinger of the coming change of seasons. The *Yukon Queen* was a week out of Circle City. Another week would see the riverboat in St. Michael.

So far there had been no trouble on the trip. Longarm and Joe had taken turns guarding Harrison Dodge, who seemed to have subsided into a state of deep depression and gloom. Dodge knew now that he was fated to go back to Washington and testify against the powerful men who had perpetrated the land-fraud scheme.

Things had even been peaceful among the members of the crew. Longarm had worried that there would be friction between the new members of the crew and the old ones, but so far that hadn't happened. And everyone was pleased with Muleshoe, who had turned out to be one hell of a cook.

All in all, Longarm thought as he lounged along the deck, he didn't have any complaints . . . which was worrisome as all get out. He found himself waiting for the other shoe to drop. He was sure that when it did, it would land on him, and whoever was wearing it would have stepped in shit recently.

"Custis."

The quiet voice broke him out of his reverie. He looked

up to see Kate Ridgway standing in the open doorway of one of the cabins. He hadn't realized he was in front of her cabin.

He reached up and tugged on the brim of his Stetson. "Evenin', Kate," he said. He hadn't talked to her very often since the boat left Circle City. Since he was no longer the first mate, he didn't spend any time in the wheelhouse. That was Ben McConnell's job now.

He sort of missed those hours he'd spent watching the river and talking to Kate. If his life had worked out differently, that wouldn't have been a bad way to spend the rest of it.

"Glad I ran into you," he went on.

"It wasn't an accident," Kate said. "I know you take a walk around the deck every night about this time before you turn in."

Longarm shrugged. "Habit, I reckon. I got used to making sure everything was squared away while we were on our way upriver to Circle City."

"You made a fine first mate," Kate said.

"McConnell's a better one. Seems like he was born and bred to the river."

"Ben's a good riverman . . . and a good man." Kate stepped closer to him. She was wearing her boots, tight whipcord trousers, and a white shirt open at the throat. It was open even more than usual, Longarm noted, enough so that the top of the dark valley between her breasts was revealed. She said, "You're a good man, too, Custis."

Longarm considered for a moment, then said, "I may be a damned fool for bringin' this up, but I thought you were a mite peeved at me, Kate."

"Muleshoe and I were talking, and he said that you were just doing your job. He said I shouldn't be angry with you for that. I couldn't argue with him, Custis."

So the old codger was trying to play Cupid and patch things up between him and Kate, Longarm thought. He wasn't sure if he ought to go find the old man, shake his hand and thank him, or kick his scrawny ass. McConnell had

warned Longarm to stay away from Kate, and despite the fact that trouble seemed to find him all too often, Longarm wasn't really the sort who went looking for it.

On the other hand, he never had cared for being told what to do, either . . .

"You better be sure you know what you're doing, Kate," he said quietly.

"I always know what I'm doing," she said as she came even closer to him. She put up a hand, touched his rugged face. Longarm felt the heat coming off her body, only inches away from his now.

The hell with it, he decided. He put his arms around her and kissed her.

Her lips opened immediately to allow his tongue to delve into her mouth. Her body sagged against his as she wound her arms around his neck. Longarm's manhood began to rise as he felt the soft pressure of Kate's groin.

After a moment, she broke the kiss and whispered, "In my cabin."

Longarm nodded. He didn't pause to give any thought to McConnell's whereabouts as he followed her into the cabin and she shut the door behind them. He never had believed in sneaking around. If McConnell found out about what was going on, then so be it.

A lamp burned on the small table beside Kate's bunk, its wick turned down low so that only a soft yellow glow filled the cabin. Longarm took off his hat and his sheepskin jacket and set them aside, then Kate stepped up to him and started unbuttoning his shirt. He returned the favor. When he spread her shirt open, it revealed full, heavy breasts crowned with dark brown nipples. Longarm filled his hands with the soft, creamy globes of woman flesh and ran his thumbs over their hardened buds. Kate moaned, soft and low and deep in her throat.

She stripped Longarm's shirt off as he fondled her breasts, then whispered for him to stop long enough to allow her to peel off the top half of his long underwear. When that was done, he finished taking the shirt off of her, so that they were

156

both nude from the waist up. He cupped her breasts again as she ran her fingers through the mat of dark brown hair on his broad, muscular chest. Her fingers dug in, feeling the strength of his body.

Kate's lips were parted and her breath was quickening as she reached down to unfasten Longarm's belt and the buttons on his denim trousers. He took off his gun belt and reached over to place it on the table near the lamp. Kate pushed Longarm's trousers down over his hips, then hooked her fingers in the waistband of his underwear and pulled it down as well. Longarm's shaft, long and thick and hard, sprang up eagerly as it was freed.

Nude from the waist up but still wearing her trousers and boots, Kate knelt in front of him and took the head of his organ into her mouth. An exquisite throb went through the pole of male flesh as her soft, hot lips closed around it. She reached behind him with both hands and dug her fingers into the cheeks of his rump, holding him steady as she gradually swallowed more and more of his shaft. Her mouth stretched wide as she took it in.

Longarm had had French lessons from gals all over the West, but it took only a moment for him to realize that Kate Ridgway was one of the best at it. She sucked him with an eagerness and enthusiasm that almost had him spilling his seed in her mouth right away. He controlled the impulse, however, unwilling to have this encounter over with so soon.

With his eyes closed, he enjoyed the sensations Kate was arousing in him for a few more minutes, then took hold of her bare shoulders and pulled her up to face him. He kissed her hard, tonguing her again. She gave as good as she got, circling his tongue with her own and thrusting it into his mouth.

She started backing up toward the bunk. Longarm went with her and lowered her to the blankets. He stepped back, kicking off his boots, trousers, and underwear while she watched from the bunk, her magnificent breasts rising and falling quickly. Once he was naked, Longarm came back to her and lifted her right leg. He took off the boot and tossed

it aside, then did the same with the boot on her left foot. Kate unfastened her trousers, and Longarm pulled them off her legs. That left her in the bottom half of a pair of long underwear. He reached under her rump to get hold of them and peeled them off her as well. Now they were both nude.

Longarm took hold of her calves and lifted her legs, bringing them up and back so that they were doubled against her. That made the thickly furred slot between her legs prominent and easy to reach. Longarm used his fingers to spread the moist folds of feminine flesh, opening Kate's womanhood like the blossoming of a flower. He went to his knees beside the bunk and leaned forward to run his tongue along the opening. She gave a low, breathy cry of passion.

Longarm turned his head a little so that he could slide his tongue inside her. She moaned at this intimate oral caress. His saliva and her natural juices blended so that her womanhood was drenched. The lips of the opening quivered slightly as they spread open, waiting anxiously for what was to come.

Finally, Longarm lifted his head from her core and moved over her. He was so hard and ready that his shaft was like a bar of iron. Kate reached down to grasp it and brought the tip to the gates of her femininity. With only a slight thrust of his hips, he slid into her, sheathing himself fully within the hot, steamy grotto.

Kate put her arms around him and clutched him with an incredible strength born of the passion and desire she was experiencing. Longarm felt the same thing. His hips rose and fell as he pistoned in and out of her. She matched him thrust for thrust, both of them falling into the same steady, natural rhythm.

Longarm let himself go, more than willing at this moment to shut out the rest of the world. There was no one but him and Kate, and that was the way he wanted it. The sensations inside him built and built and finally reached the breaking point. He drove as deeply as he could into Kate and felt her began to spasm, too, as her climax gripped her. He emptied himself into her in a fevered series of shattering explosions.

His seed filled her and flowed out of her tightly clasping sheath to coat both of them. Longarm sagged atop her as his muscles all involuntarily relaxed, but somehow he still had the presence of mind to take some of his weight on his elbows so that his rangy, powerful form wouldn't crush her into the bunk.

She murmured a wordless expression of pleasure and contentment as she lingeringly caressed his back and hips and buttocks. She kissed his ear, his cheek, his jaw, his throat. Longarm kissed her shoulder, then turned his head so that he could find her mouth with his.

"That was . . . better than I ever dreamed it would be," she finally whispered. "Custis, I . . . I don't know what to say."

"I don't reckon you have to say anything," he told her. "What just happened says it better than anything else."

She nodded in agreement and hugged him. In a shaky voice, she asked, "You have to go back to your cabin now, don't you?"

"Joe's expecting me to take over guarding Dodge. If I don't show up, he's liable to send somebody to look for me." Longarm raised himself so that he could toy with one of Kate's breasts.

She clasped his hand, pressed it against her for a moment, then said, "Go on. It's all right."

"You're sure?"

"We both have our jobs, Custis, and we're good at what we do. What happened between us—it doesn't change that."

"No," Longarm agreed, "I reckon it doesn't." He bent his head quickly and kissed her again, then rolled off the bunk and reached for his clothes.

Sometimes, he thought, it would be nice if a fella could sort of freeze time and keep everything the same for a while. If the world could just wait and mind its own business for a spell, so that a man and a woman could be together without having to worry about anything else . . .

It was too damned bad that wasn't going to happen.

*　　*　　*

Longarm left his cabin early the next morning right after the riverboat shoved off from where it had been tied up for the night. He intended to go to the galley and fetch some breakfast back for the prisoner. But as soon as he stepped out onto the deck, he found Ben McConnell waiting for him.

And it took only one look at McConnell's face to know that he was in for trouble. The big redhead looked like he was fixing to cloud up and rain all over Longarm. It didn't require a genius to figure out what McConnell was upset about.

"Hold it right there, Long," McConnell snapped. "One of the boys told me he saw you slipping out of Kate's cabin last night."

"Is that so?" Longarm said coolly. "Some fellas have a habit of talking too much and not minding their own business."

McConnell's jaw tightened. "So you don't deny it?"

Longarm's eyes narrowed as he said, "I don't owe you any answers or any explanations, McConnell."

"You bastard!" the redhead burst out. "I told you to stay away from Kate!"

"I ain't a member of the crew no more, and when I was, you weren't. I don't take orders from you."

McConnell's hands clenched into fists as he stepped forward. "You'll damned well wish you had!"

"Before you take a swing, old son, you'd better remember that I'm a federal lawman."

"Maybe so, but I didn't think you were the sort to hide behind a badge," McConnell said with a sneer.

He was right about that, Longarm told himself. And he could see now that there wasn't going to be any avoiding this trouble. In that case, it might be better to get it over with.

Joe appeared in the doorway of the cabin behind Longarm, his rifle cradled in his arms. "There a problem out here, Marshal?" he asked.

"Nope," Longarm replied. He reached down, unbuckled his gun belt, and turned half around to hand the cross-draw

rig to Joe. "Hang on to this for me, will you? And keep an eye on Dodge?"

"Sure," Joe said with a grin. "I've got a hunch I'm going to miss something, though."

Longarm turned back to McConnell and jerked his head toward the stern. "Down there," he said. "That open area in front of the paddlewheel."

"That'll do," McConnell agreed.

Seeing their grim faces as they strode past, passengers and members of the crew realized something was about to happen and followed the two men. When Longarm and McConnell reached the space where they would clash, Longarm took off his Stetson and sheepskin jacket and laid them aside. McConnell did the same with his cap, then rolled his sleeves up a couple of turns over brawny forearms.

The men were evenly matched. McConnell was shorter, but only by an inch or two, and probably outweighed Longarm, but by no more than ten pounds. Both men showed the scars of previous battles, and as they clenched their fists and lifted their arms, they did so with the easy familiarity of born warriors.

McConnell threw the first punch, a straight right that Longarm recognized as a feint. Instead of falling for it and stepping into the sweeping left that McConnell brought around, Longarm slipped McConnell's right on his left forearm and stepped inside the roundhouse punch. He drove a short left and right into McConnell's belly. McConnell grunted in pain and surprise, grabbed Longarm's shirt with his left hand, and shoved him away. McConnell's face was pale as he moved back a couple of steps, putting a little distance between himself and Longarm.

One last try to talk some sense into McConnell's head wouldn't do any harm, Longarm decided. He said, "We don't have to do this."

"The hell we don't," McConnell snarled.

Well, that was it, Longarm thought. He would just have to beat the sense into McConnell's head instead.

A savage grin stretched McConnell's mouth. "Remember,

Long," he said. "This is the river. A fight out here means no holds barred."

Longarm nodded curtly. He had fought rivermen before.

McConnell lunged at him, arms outstretched. Longarm expected the move, but the first mate was so fast that he couldn't completely avoid it. McConnell's right arm went around his waist, and Longarm was forced backward by the strength of McConnell's barreling charge. His back slammed into the wall of the cabins, knocking the breath out of him for a second.

Longarm hooked a left into McConnell's belly, hoping to keep the man off him long enough to recover some of the air that had been driven out of his lungs. He whipped a backhanded right across McConnell's face. McConnell's right fist thudded into Longarm's breastbone. McConnell crowded against him, bringing up his right forearm and jamming it under Longarm's chin. That forced Longarm's head back so that his skull smacked against the wall.

The men who had gathered around to watch the fight were shouting and cheering now. Instinct wouldn't allow them to do anything else. Longarm was vaguely aware of the racket, but the roaring in his ears was even louder as McConnell's arm pressed across his throat and kept him from breathing. His body was already starved for air. A red mist began to float in from the edges of his vision.

Longarm jerked up his right knee. McConnell felt the move and twisted aside, sure that Longarm intended to smash the knee into his groin. But Longarm stopped and grabbed McConnell's left arm instead, wrapping his fingers around the wrist and wrenching it up behind McConnell's back. McConnell cried out in pain as his bones were suddenly grinding in their sockets.

The awful pressure went away from Longarm's throat. As he gasped for air, he twisted McConnell's arm some more and then pushed the first mate away from him. McConnell staggered, caught his balance against the rail, and swung back toward Longarm. Longarm could have used a few seconds to recover, but he knew he wasn't going to get that

162

respite. As McConnell turned, Longarm met him with a hard right to the jaw.

The blow threw McConnell against the rail again, and now it was Longarm's turn to crowd his opponent. He stepped in, putting all the power of his arms and shoulders into the punches he drove into McConnell's body. McConnell gasped and tried to avoid the blows, but Longarm had him pinned against the rail just in front of the paddlewheel. There was nowhere for him to go. Spray came off the steadily turning wheel and misted over both men as they fought in its shadow.

McConnell threw a wild, lucky punch that grazed Longarm's head with enough power to knock him back a step. McConnell lowered his own head and bulled forward, crashing into Longarm and butting him in the stomach. Longarm couldn't stay on his feet in the face of that charge. He went over backward, his shoulders slamming into the planks of the deck.

But even as he fell, he got his right leg up and planted his boot in McConnell's midsection. Longarm used McConnell's own momentum against him then, levering the first mate up and over so that he flew through the air and smashed into the wall of the cabins. He dropped half-senseless to the deck as Longarm rolled over and struggled onto hands and knees.

Longarm hoped that McConnell had been knocked out, but he saw that wasn't the case. McConnell was fighting to get up, too, shaking his head as if to clear away cobwebs in his brain. The chests of both men were heaving as they finally staggered to their feet.

From the start, there had been nothing fancy about this fight, but now it descended to an even more barbaric level. Longarm and McConnell came together, standing toe to toe and slugging it out with sweeping blows that rocked a man's head back when they landed. Now the chances for victory rode on which man could absorb the most punishment while still dishing it out.

Longarm's arms were heavy as lead as he lifted them and struck at McConnell again and again. McConnell's punches thudded into his body, but Longarm barely felt them. The

pounding he'd already received had numbed him all over. His brain was numb, too, unable to think of any fancy moves he might have made to end the fight. He was lucky that McConnell was in just as bad a shape, if not worse.

There was no telling how long they might have stood there flailing away at each other if the sudden roar of a shot hadn't blasted through the air. The explosion of the gun silenced the crowd of onlookers. Longarm and McConnell didn't react right away. Each man swung a final punch as the second barrel of the shotgun cut loose. Both blows missed, and Longarm and McConnell wound up stumbling forward and running into each other. They stayed there like that, sort of propped on each other so that they didn't fall down, as their heads slowly swiveled around to see who was shooting.

"Have you two gone crazy?" Kate demanded. Smoke still curled from the twin barrels of the shotgun she held. She thrust the weapon into the hands of one of the bystanders and stalked forward to confront Longarm and McConnell. She raged, "Don't think I don't know why you two lunkheads are fighting!"

"Katie . . ." McConnell said thickly through swollen lips.

"Don't call me that!"

McConnell spat blood onto the deck. "All right then— Cap'n. Long had it comin'. I told him—"

"I don't care what you told him. He's a passenger on this boat now, and you're the first mate. I won't have you brawling with the passengers."

Longarm dabbed with his fingers at the blood leaking from a cut on his cheek. He said, "Don't be too hard on him, Kate—"

She turned toward him and interrupted. "And you! I thought you had more sense."

Longarm blinked. "Kate, I—"

McConnell said, "He had no right—"

"Shut up, both of you!" Glaring at them in disgust and contempt, Kate started to turn away.

McConnell lunged after her and caught hold of her arm, stopping her. "Damn it, Kate, listen to me! How do you

reckon it makes me feel when I find out that you and him ... that you ... that he—"

"Why should anything I do make you feel anything?" Kate demanded coldly.

"Because I love you, damn it!"

If McConnell expected that declaration to melt her rage, he was in for a disappointment. She kept glaring at him and snapped, "Well, you've got a piss-poor way of showing it, mister!"

He still had hold of her arm. Now he grabbed her other one and jerked her against him. He brought his mouth down on hers, then winced as the kiss hurt his bruised lips. But he didn't pull away.

Muleshoe Flynn stepped over to Longarm and nudged him in the side with an elbow. "You goin' to let him get away with that?"

Longarm grinned wearily. "Looks like she's the one lettin' him get away with it. If Kate don't mind, I don't reckon I got any right to object."

Muleshoe spat on the deck and shook his head. "Sometimes I just can't figure you young fellers out."

Kate and McConnell were still kissing as Longarm forced his aching muscles into motion and picked up his hat and coat. He had known, even as he was bedding Kate the night before, that what was between them was nothing permanent. Alaska was her home, and he had to return to his job in Denver. McConnell was the man for her.

But if they hadn't given in to the temptation of the moment, they always would have wondered—and regretted— what they might have missed. There were enough regrets in Longarm's life. He didn't need any more.

"Come on, Muleshoe," he said. "A ruckus like that before breakfast always gives me a hell of an appetite."

Chapter 14

By the next day, Longarm was sore all over from the battle royal with McConnell. From what he had seen of the two of them together, however, McConnell and Kate had resolved their differences, and he was glad of that.

Not that everything was peaches-and-cream between them, Longarm reflected with a grin as he walked along the deck and heard them arguing in the wheelhouse. They were both mighty strong willed, and any relationship they had was likely to be stormy. But after the storms would come the tranquil times, and then it would all be worth it.

He returned to the cabin and spelled Joe from guard duty. After Joe left, Longarm straddled a chair and looked at Harrison Dodge, who was still tied into another chair. They untied him only for meals and when he needed to relieve himself.

Longarm took out a cheroot and lit it. "I been thinking, Dodge," he said. "What made a fella like you decide to get mixed up in that land fraud? You never were a crook before."

Dodge looked at him dully, and for a moment Longarm thought the man wasn't going to answer. Then Dodge said, "Of course I wasn't a criminal. I've always been an honest man."

"But you falsified government land deeds and other documents."

A little life came back into Dodge's eyes. "I had to," he said fiercely. "They didn't give me any choice. They . . . they said they'd kill me if I didn't help them."

Longarm frowned as he puffed on the cheroot. "You're sayin' you were forced into being part of the scheme?"

"That's right."

"Why should I believe you, old son?"

Dodge laughed, and there was an edge of hysteria in the sound. "What purpose would there be in lying to you now?"

Longarm pondered that and shrugged.

"I'm not a brave man," Dodge went on. "I just wanted to save my life, so I went along with him when he approached me. I knew right away that I . . . I had to cooperate, or he'd have me killed."

"Who?" Longarm asked. "Who was behind it, Dodge?" It wasn't his job to get that information out of Dodge, but it wouldn't hurt to know it, either. And Billy Vail hadn't told him *not* to question the fugitive.

Dodge just shook his head. "I won't say. You can take me back, and they can send me to prison, but I won't say. My life would never be worth anything if I did."

For the first time in this case, Longarm felt a little sorry for the man he had pursued all the way into the Alaskan wilderness. Dodge had been going along living his drab, colorless life, but that life was still precious to him. Suddenly, it had been threatened by the greed of another man, a powerful man who clearly wouldn't hesitate at anything to get what he wanted. That man would have squashed Dodge like a bug if Dodge had refused to cooperate with him.

It wasn't his job to make judgments like that, Longarm reminded himself. Whatever Dodge had to say, it was between him and the authorities back in Washington.

The *Yukon Queen* had already passed the spot where the river pirates had laid their trap on the voyage to Circle City. Longarm had been alert for any sign of the pirates, but so far the trip had been peaceful. He looked up in surprise as he heard the steam whistle on the boat's smokestack blow. "Wonder what that's about?" he muttered. He would have

167

gone and checked, but he didn't want to leave Dodge alone.

Joe solved that problem for him a moment later by opening the door and saying, "Cap'n Ridgway wants you up in the wheelhouse, Marshal. I'll watch the prisoner."

"Thanks, Joe," Longarm said as he stood up and moved to the door. Worry gnawed at his vitals. After coming this far, he didn't want anything to threaten his assignment now.

He went up the ladder and stepped inside the wheelhouse, and as he did he looked down the river and saw the other steamboat coming toward them. Kate looked over her shoulder and smiled at him. "There's the *Samuel Jennings*, on her way to Circle City," she said. "I know you were worried about Grantham and Swain coming after us, so I thought you'd like to know that it'll still be a couple of weeks before the *Jennings* reaches Circle City. You'll be well on your way back to San Francisco before those two can get to St. Michael."

Longarm nodded. It was good to know, all right. "You normally blow your whistle when you meet another boat?"

"Sometimes. It's just a way of saying hello."

Longarm eyed McConnell, who stood beside the chart table watching Longarm warily. The first mate was as battered and bruised as Longarm himself was. Of all the people on board, Longarm reflected, McConnell would be just as glad as any of them to reach St. Michael. Once Longarm had sailed away, McConnell could stop worrying about him competing for Kate's affections.

He could stop that already, Longarm thought, only he didn't know it and likely wouldn't believe it if Longarm had told him. As pleasant as the interlude with Kate had been, that was all it was.

The *Samuel Jennings* was closer now, no more than a hundred yards downriver. Her captain blew a blast on the whistle, and Kate returned it. She leaned forward over the wheel to wave at the other vessel, but the gesture died before it began. Instead she frowned suddenly and said, "What's that boat doing?"

"Changing course," McConnell answered. "Damn it, they're going to crowd us."

Longarm peered out the wheelhouse windows and saw that McConnell was right. If the *Samuel Jennings* had maintained its original course, it would have passed a good fifty yards to port of the *Yukon Queen*. Instead, the bow of the second sternwheeler was now swinging sharply toward the middle of the river, which meant it was angling toward the *Yukon Queen*.

"Has that captain lost his mind?" Kate muttered.

"Hard starboard!" McConnell exclaimed. "The bastard's trying to ram us, Kate!"

Kate's eyes widened as she realized that McConnell was right. She spun the wheel desperately, trying to move the *Yukon Queen* out of the path of the onrushing *Samuel Jennings*. Black smoke billowed out of the *Jennings*'s stack as its engineer poured on the power to the engines.

Longarm could think of only one reason the other riverboat would try to wreck the *Yukon Queen*: it was no longer under the command of its regular captain but had been taken over by someone who wanted to stop the *Yukon Queen* at all costs.

So it came as no surprise when, as the boats rushed toward each other, he spotted Raymond Grantham and Timothy Swain crouched on the bow of the *Jennings*, each of them holding a rifle.

Longarm's jaw clenched tightly. That bastard Bert Truman must have taken a payoff to go back on his word to Longarm and release the two prisoners early. Then Grantham and Swain had somehow gotten downriver ahead of the *Yukon Queen* and taken over the *Samuel Jennings*. To do that, they would have had to have help. Longarm didn't know all the details, but that wasn't really important now. All that mattered was that the other riverboat was looming closer and closer as Kate tried desperately to get her vessel out of the way.

Coils of smoke blossomed from the men on the deck of the *Jennings*. They were shooting, Longarm realized. A sec-

169

ond later a bullet whined through the wheelhouse. "Kate, get down!" McConnell cried.

"I'm not leaving the wheel, damn it!" she bit back at him. "I need more power!"

McConnell grabbed the speaking tube and yelled down to the engine room for more power, then dropped the rubber tube and threw himself at Kate. His arms went around her and jerked her away from the wheel. She cried out as both of them fell to the floor. At that instant, a slug smacked into the wheel and chewed splinters from it.

It didn't matter whether Kate was at the wheel or not, Longarm realized as he spun toward the door. The suicidal charge of the *Samuel Jennings* could not be avoided. "Brace yourselves!" he bellowed to the confused passengers and crew on the deck. "We're gonna hit!"

A couple of heartbeats later, with a huge, grinding crash, that was exactly what happened. Kate had managed to turn the riverboat so that the collision wasn't bow to bow, but the port side of the *Jennings* still slammed into the port side of the *Yukon Queen*. With a shudder that shook both boats, they scraped roughly together.

Longarm ignored the ladder and dropped to the main deck, going to one knee before he could catch his balance. The two boats seemed to have been locked together by the crash, and men were leaping from the deck of the *Jennings* onto the *Yukon Queen*. Guns barked and boomed, and men cursed and cried out in pain.

The boarders were hard-faced men in fur coats and caps. The river pirates had struck again, Longarm realized as he palmed out his Colt. Somehow, Grantham and Swain had fallen in with the gang of brigands, probably promising them a big payoff if they helped the two assassins stop the riverboat. Longarm brought up his revolver as one of the pirates rushed him. He triggered once, the slug driving into the attacker's chest and sending him flying off the boat into the river.

Longarm turned and raced along the deck toward the cabin where Dodge was being held. He had to protect the prisoner.

As he neared the cabin, one of the pirates reached the door and kicked it open. Before the man could swarm into the room, a rifle blasted and kicked the pirate back across the deck. He hit the rail, flipped over it, and plunged into the Yukon.

Longarm stopped outside the door. "Joe!" he shouted. "You all right?"

"All right, Marshal!" the reply came.

"Use my Winchester. Hold 'em off as best you can."

"Yes, sir!"

"And get Dodge down on the floor!"

With Joe holding down the fort here, Longarm was free to try to turn the tide of battle. The pirates weren't finding it easy to take over the *Yukon Queen*. The crew was a salty bunch, and many of the passengers were hardened frontiersmen, too. Guns banged all over the boat. Longarm circled the cabins and started back toward the bow.

A big, bearded man seemed to be in charge of the raiders. He was bellowing orders and waving the pirates forward as he stood on the bow of the *Jennings*. He had a Winchester in his hand, and as he spotted Longarm he lifted the rifle and aimed it like a pistol.

Longarm got his shots off first, triggering the Colt twice. The rifle in the big pirate's hand blasted, but the shot went wild as Longarm's bullets kicked up puffs of dust from the breast of the fur coat the man was wearing. The pirate leader swayed as the rifle he held drooped, and then he toppled forward like a falling tree, landing on the deck of the *Yukon Queen*.

When the pirate fell, the man who had been standing behind him was revealed. It was Bert Truman, the storekeeper from Circle City, and the sight of him confirmed Longarm's guess. Truman was probably part of the gang, selling the goods that the pirates stole from the riverboats. He had a pistol in his hand, and as he ducked for cover behind a barrel, he snapped a couple of shots toward Longarm.

Longarm ignored the bullets whipping past his head and aimed carefully at the barrel, firing twice. The slugs punched

through the barrel, throwing shards of wood in the air. For a second, Longarm couldn't tell if the bullets had gone all the way through or not, but then Bert Truman swayed slowly into sight and sprawled onto the deck of the commandeered riverboat, blood spreading in a pool around him.

As was the habit of anyone who regularly carried a gun, Longarm kept an empty chamber in the Colt's cylinder for the hammer to rest on. That meant his revolver was now empty. He ducked back in an alcove and reached into the pocket of his sheepskin jacket for more cartridges. It took him only a few seconds to dump his empty brass and thumb fresh rounds into the Colt's cylinder.

This time he loaded all six chambers.

His head jerked up as he heard a scream from the wheelhouse. Even over the rattle of gunfire, the shrill sound knifed through the air.

Kate!

Longarm burst out of his temporary shelter. Bullets chopped into the deck around his feet as he ran for the closest ladder. Just as he reached it, one of the pirates leaped across from the *Jennings* and lunged at his back, swinging a huge hunting knife.

Longarm saw the man from the corner of his eye and tried to turn, with a sickening feeling in his stomach that he was going to be too late. Then an explosion went off almost in his face, deafening him momentarily. As he caught hold of a ladder rung with his free hand to keep himself from falling, he saw Muleshoe Flynn standing a couple of feet away with a wreath of powdersmoke around his whiskery face. The smoke came from the barrel of Muleshoe's old hogleg, which he had just used to blow a fist-sized hole through the pirate behind Longarm.

"See to the cap'n!" Muleshoe cried with a gleeful cackle. "I'll cover your back!"

Longarm jammed his Colt in its holster so that he could use both hands on the ladder. He swarmed up it to the roof of the cabins. When he reached the top, he saw Yak standing toward the stern, firing down into the mass of struggling men

on the deck. Bloodstains streaked the old Indian's shirt, but he was grinning and seemed to be having the time of his life, just like Muleshoe.

Longarm plunged toward the wheelhouse, and as he approached a figure came stumbling out the door. Longarm caught hold of Ben McConnell's arm before the big redhead could fall. "Knifed me—" McConnell grated. "The . . . son of a bitch . . . !"

Longarm saw someone struggling with Kate inside the wheelhouse. He couldn't risk a shot because the river pirate was so close to her. Then McConnell jerked loose from his grip, and knife wound or no knife wound, flung himself through the door and back into the fight.

Longarm saw a hand holding a knife go up. Kate grabbed the man's wrist with both hands to hold off the blade. Then McConnell crashed into them and got his arms around the pirate's neck. McConnell yanked back, hauling the man away from Kate. As they struggled, they turned toward Longarm, and he was surprised to see the face of Ike Carpen. Carpen's features were turning a dark red as he struggled for air against the choking hold that McConnell had on him. He tried to slash behind him with the knife, but from this angle, he couldn't reach McConnell.

Suddenly McConnell braced his feet and poured all his strength into his arms and shoulders. Muscles bunched and corded and stood out against the tight fabric of his shirt. A loud cracking noise resounded through the wheelhouse. Longarm saw Carpen's eyes go glassy and knew that McConnell had just broken his neck.

With Kate safe—for the time being—Longarm turned his attention back to the attackers. The river pirates had found a lot more resistance on the *Yukon Queen* than they must have expected. The gunfire was dying away now, as the remaining struggles were more hand-to-hand.

Longarm became aware that the deck was shuddering under his feet, but not from the engines of the *Yukon Queen*, which had gone quiet. Whoever was down in the engine room must have shut them off after the crash.

But the same wasn't true for the *Samuel Jennings*. Black smoke still poured from the other riverboat's stack. The *Jennings* was shaking violently as it shoved the *Yukon Queen* toward the shore.

The pirates had pushed the boilers of the stolen riverboat for all the power they could get, and then they probably had left the engine room to get in on the attack. If those boilers were unattended, Longarm thought, but still building up steam . . .

"Kate!" he shouted. "We've got to get free from that other boat!"

Inside the wheelhouse, the body of Ike Carpen had slumped to the floor when McConnell finally released him. McConnell and Kate both looked out the window at the *Samuel Jennings*, and experienced as they were with riverboats, they understood the danger instantly. McConnell lurched out of the wheelhouse, still ignoring the knife wound in his side.

"Come on!" he called to Longarm.

Some of the pirates, seeing how the fight was going, were now abandoning the *Yukon Queen*. They jumped off and swam for the shore, preferring to take their chances in the frigid Yukon River. As Longarm and McConnell reached the deck, Longarm spotted Carl and Pete and called to them, "Grab those poles!"

The young men snatched up the long poles used for shoving off and followed Longarm and McConnell around the bow to the port side of the boat. Longarm and McConnell took one of the poles while Pete and Carl took the other. They planted the tips of the poles against the hull of the *Jennings* and began to push. McConnell turned his head and bellowed over his shoulder up to the wheelhouse, "Back full on the engines, Kate!"

The big paddlewheel at the stern, which had been still, slowly began to turn again. It bit at the water, sending shudders through the boat as it tried to pull free from the doomed *Jennings*. Longarm and the others threw all their strength against the poles.

Fleetingly, Longarm wondered what had happened to

Grantham and Swain. From the corner of his eye he suddenly spotted them jumping from the *Yukon Queen* to the deck of the *Jennings*. Between them they gripped a smaller figure— Harrison Dodge.

"Son of a bitch!" Longarm grated. He didn't know why they hadn't just killed Dodge outright. But he knew he couldn't let them escape with the man.

"Yak! Muleshoe!" he shouted, seeing the two old-timers nearby. "Grab this pole!"

They moved to take his place as McConnell and the others continued trying to break the two riverboats apart. With a loud grinding and scraping, the *Yukon Queen* suddenly came free, just as Longarm leaped from its deck to the *Samuel Jennings*. The unexpected lurch threw him off-balance when he landed, and he fell forward.

That probably saved his life, because at that instant Timothy Swain let loose a shot at him from halfway along the deck. Sprawled on his belly, Longarm returned the fire and saw Swain spin around as the bullets tore into his body. Swain dropped his gun and slumped against the wall of the cabins, sliding down slowly to the deck and leaving a smear of blood behind him.

Longarm surged to his feet, looking for Grantham and Dodge. He didn't see them. Grantham must have retreated either into one of the cabins or back toward the stern, where the paddlewheel was revolving madly. The *Jennings* was out of control now, and as Longarm glanced up at the wheelhouse, he saw that no one was there. The boat was steaming toward the shore of the river. The question was whether it would crash first, or if the boilers would explode and blow the vessel into kindling before that could happen.

Longarm started along the deck, alert for any sign of Grantham, and a flicker of movement from the stern warned him in time for him to twist aside as a gun barked. The bullet whined past him. Longarm flattened himself against the wall of the cabins.

"Grantham!" he shouted. "This boat's gonna blow to

Kingdom Come, Grantham! Throw down your gun and let's get off it before that happens!"

"Go to hell, Long!" Grantham yelled back at him. "You get off the boat, or I'll kill Dodge!"

Longarm still didn't know why Grantham hadn't already done that, but he got his answer a moment later as Grantham edged into view, one arm looped around Dodge's neck while the other hand pressed the barrel of a pistol to the little man's head.

"I don't want to shoot him, Long, because he's worth more to me alive than dead," Grantham said, "but I will if I have to!"

Longarm took a step away from the wall, keeping his Colt leveled. "You figuring on doing a little blackmail, Grantham?" he asked, raising his voice so that it could be heard over the labored roar of the engines. "You don't think Dodge's boss will let you get away with that, do you? He'll just send somebody else to kill *you*."

"I'm too smart to let that happen," Grantham boasted. "I fooled you, didn't I?"

"Yeah, old son, I reckon you did. But this is the end of the line."

Glaring at Longarm over Dodge's shoulder, Grantham shook his head. "No," he insisted. "I'm still going to win. I'm going to be a rich man because of this terrified little mouse."

Dodge's eyes opened wide, and he suddenly drove his elbow back into Grantham's midsection. The blow took Grantham by surprise, and Dodge was able to jerk his head away from the barrel of the gun before Grantham could pull the trigger. Grantham fired anyway. Dodge cried out in pain as specks of blazing powder burned the side of his face, but the bullet missed him. He kicked back against Grantham's shin and threw himself forward at the same time, breaking free and falling to the deck.

The deck was jumping under Longarm's feet like an earthquake now. He steadied himself as best he could and fired as Grantham tried to bring the revolver around toward him.

The slug from Longarm's gun hit Grantham just below the breastbone and knocked him back. He staggered and tried to catch his balance, then hit the railing at the stern of the riverboat. With a scream, he toppled over it, falling into the paddlewheel that was spinning so fast it was only a blur. Grantham's shriek was lost in the high-pitched whine of every safety valve in the engine room of the *Jennings* blowing out at once. The noise filled the air like the cry of a banshee.

Longarm lunged toward Dodge, who was trying to get shakily to his feet. Dodge yelped in surprise as Longarm grabbed him and bulled both of them toward the rail. They went up and over and into the river, and Longarm kicked his feet hard, hanging on to Dodge and driving them both as deep into the water as he could.

The fiery explosion threw pieces of the *Samuel Jennings* hundreds of feet into the air. The debris pattered back down seconds later, falling into the Yukon with tiny splashes. The shattered hulk of the riverboat, furiously ablaze, drifted closer to shore.

Longarm's head broke the surface. He gasped for air and struck out for the river bank, towing Harrison Dodge behind him.

He couldn't tell for sure, but he had the horrible feeling that he was towing dead weight.

Chapter 15

The air inside the meeting room in the United States Capitol Building was musty and overly warm from the fire burning in the stove in the corner. Outside, an autumn storm had large, fragile snowflakes swirling around the impressive structure.

Longarm wished he was outside in the snow. He didn't like Washington, liked even less being shut up in here with these stuffed shirts. He reached up and tugged at his collar.

Billy Vail leaned over and whispered, "Stop fidgeting, Custis. They'll get to you in a minute."

Senator Tobias Culp was droning on about something. The senator, a stocky man with a white, spade beard, was conducting this hearing into the land-fraud scandal that had rocked Washington. Several officials high in the Interior Department had resigned and faced possible criminal charges. Secretary Schurz appeared to be safe, since no evidence had come up linking him with the scheme, but the whole thing was still the talk of the town.

Longarm became aware that Senator Culp was talking to Billy Vail. The chief marshal for the Western District rose to his feet and said, "Yes, sir, Senator, we have one item to offer into evidence."

Culp frowned. "I was given to understand, Marshal, that the witness you were charged with locating and bringing

back here for this hearing met an unfortunate demise."

"Yes, sir, he did," Vail agreed. "But we still have some evidence."

"Well, then," Culp said testily, "let's see it."

Vail turned to Longarm and said, "Custis."

Longarm stood up. The hearing was well-attended, with quite a few newspaper reporters seated in the back of the meeting room. He heard a few of them muttering as he strode forward toward the table where Culp and five other senators were sitting. He knew he looked a mite out of place here— but not as out of place as he felt.

As he came to a stop in front of the table, Culp looked up at him from narrowed eyes and said, "Well? Just who are you, son?"

"Deputy U.S. Marshal Custis Long, Senator," Longarm introduced himself. "I'm the one who was supposed to fetch Harrison Dodge back here."

"And you failed in that task," Culp said severely.

"Yes, sir, I reckon I did."

One of the journalists snickered at Longarm's Western accent. He ignored the flash of irritation he felt. What was happening here was too important for him to lose his temper.

"Then what can you offer us, Marshal, since the witness is deceased?"

Longarm reached inside his coat and took out a thin, leather-bound book. "This here, Senator," he said as he placed the volume on the table in front of Culp. "The written testimony of the late Harrison Dodge. This journal tells everything Dodge knew about the land fraud, including the name of the gent who came up with the scheme in the first place."

Culp blinked. "This . . . this is very irregular," he sputtered. "How do we know that Dodge even wrote this so-called journal?"

"He worked for the government as a clerk," Longarm drawled. "I reckon there's plenty of samples of his writing around here. You can compare it for yourself."

One of the other senators leaned forward. "Written testi-

mony must be given and sworn to in front of some sort of competent authority."

"Yes, sir," Longarm said with a nod. "I got an affidavit here from Grover Hanratty, the mayor of St. Michael, Alaska Territory, stating that in his presence Harrison Dodge wrote what's in this book in his own hand before passin' away from the injuries he received in the explosion that destroyed the riverboat *Samuel Jennings*."

"Explosion!" another senator exclaimed. "This is the first I've heard of an explosion."

Longarm nodded again. "Yes, sir, that boat blew up right after Dodge and me jumped off it. I can tell you the whole story if you'd like, all about how the fella behind the land fraud sent some killers after Dodge. They murdered a gal here in Washington first, though, a ladyfriend of Dodge's."

"This is incredible. From the way you talk, Marshal, there was a . . . a web of wickedness spanning practically the entire continent."

"Yep," Longarm agreed. "And there was one man behind all of it." He turned and looked straight at Culp. "Ain't that right, Senator?"

Culp swallowed and reached for the journal of Harrison Dodge. "This is absurd! This so-called evidence is meaningless—"

Longarm's hand came down onto the slender book. "This ain't a trial, it's just a hearing. What say I pick up this book and let these other senators hear what's wrote down in it?"

Culp was pale and sweating by now, and it wasn't from the heat in the room, Longarm thought. Culp said, "It . . . it's a pack of lies. Damned, despicable lies!"

"How do you know that, Senator, when you ain't even heard yet what Dodge wrote?"

Culp stared up at Longarm. His mouth worked, but no words came out.

One of the other senators leaned forward. "I think that's enough, Marshal," he said quietly to Longarm. "If you'll give that book to me, I'll take charge of it and see that its contents are entered into the record."

With a flick of his wrist, Longarm sent the book sliding down the table. "Much obliged, Senator."

Then he turned and walked back to the table where Vail was waiting for him. Longarm picked up his hat, swallowed the taste of bitterness in his mouth, and said, "Let's get out of here, Billy."

With Vail hurrying alongside him, Longarm's long strides carried him out of the Capitol Building into the cold but clean air. Longarm paused on the steps to light a cheroot and said around the cigar, "You reckon Culp'll ever pay for all the killin' he caused, Billy?"

"I think you can count on that, Custis." Vail shook his head. "This town never fails to amaze me. It's the only place in the world they'd put a fox in charge of the henhouse."

Longarm chuckled, and together the two lawmen walked down the steps, snowflakes crunching under their boots.

More than a month earlier, downriver from the scene of the battle with the river pirates, the *Yukon Queen* had come across the survivors from the crew and passengers of the *Samuel Jennings*, who had escaped when the pirates took over the riverboat. Grantham, Swain, Truman, Ike Carpen, and the pirate leader called Breed Dixon had ridden hard downriver to get ahead of the *Yukon Queen* and intercept the *Jennings*, just as Longarm had speculated.

All the bullet holes and knife wounds had been patched up, and the damage from the collision was repaired during a layover of a couple of days at Burke's Bar. Grantham had shot Joe in the shoulder, but the young Indian was sturdy enough to recover rapidly. The same was true of Ben McConnell, who had been knifed in the side by Carpen. If anything, Longarm thought, McConnell would heal even quicker than Joe, because McConnell had Kate to nurse him back to health.

Unless they got too frisky, of course. Then McConnell would have to be careful not to tear that wound open again.

When they got back to St. Michael, Harrison Dodge wrote up his testimony implicating Senator Tobias Culp as the ar-

181

chitect of the land-fraud scheme, the man who had threatened to kill him, and the man who had tried to follow through on that threat when Dodge fled. Then, quickly, they had dug a grave in St. Michael's tiny cemetery before the ground froze too hard for the winter.

"You sure you're goin' to be all right?" Longarm had asked Dodge as they stood together in front of the wooden marker with Dodge's name carved on it.

"As long as I stay dead, I will be," Dodge replied. "Marshal, I . . . I can't tell you what it means to have a second chance like this. I know you're bending the rules . . ."

"It ain't the first time," Longarm told him. "Besides, you got dealt a bad hand. I like to set things straight when I get a chance. That don't mean I forgive you for cloutin' me on the head in that hotel, though." Longarm's grin took any sting out of the words. "Don't get too rich up there on the Yukon, hear?"

"Muleshoe assured me that his map will lead us to a fabulous treasure."

"Maybe so." Longarm shook hands with Dodge. "Good luck." He turned and walked away.

As far as he could see, being alive and having that second chance, Dodge was already getting a pretty fabulous treasure.

Watch for

**LONGARM AND THE SIDESADDLE
ASSASSIN**

278th novel in the exciting LONGARM series
from Jove

Coming in January!

LONGARM

Explore the exciting Old West with one of the men who made it wild!

J. R. ROBERTS
THE GUNSMITH

FIRE AND ICE

If there's one thing U.S. Deputy Marshal Long can't stand, it's a yeller witness who heads for the hills just when the law needs him most. Harrison Dodge is one such lily-livered sleaze. Privy to Washington's dirty secrets, Dodge realizes he knows too much—and quits the capital with a one-way ticket. Destination: anywhere.

Longarm tries to sniff out the little runt, and finds himself on a boat bound for Alaska. Unfortunately, tip-to-tip, Alaska measures only a mite smaller than the U.S. of A. His only means of transportation is a riverboat, the *Yukon Queen*, driven by a hot-tempered, fiery lady-captain. Now, not only does Longarm have to keep his eyes peeled for any sign of his fugitive, he must also help his captain ward off her enemies. And try to keep his burning desire for her from melting the Alaskan ice…

DON'T MISS OTHERS IN THE

ISBN 0-515-13206-3

13206

UPC

0 71152 00499 4